MR.
GLAMOUR

**RICHARD
GODWIN**

A Black Jackal Books Paperback
First published in Great Britain in 2012 by Black Jackal Books
Copyright © Richard Godwin 2012

ISBN 978-0-9567113-3-5

Book and cover design by Page Godwin
http://uk.linkedin.com/pub/page-godwin/47/488/124

FSC
www.fsc.org
MIX
Paper from
responsible sources
FSC® C013604

Printed by CPI Group UK
Papers used by Black Jackal Books are natural
renewable and recyclable products sourced from
well-managed forests and certified in accordance
with the rules of the Forest Stewardship Council

Black Jackal Books Ltd, Suite 106, 143 Kingston Road,
London SW19 1LJ

For William, Jelena, Nova and Page

THE GLAMOUR SET

1

She has the eyes of a pit viper and the mouth of an angel.
She parts her lips slowly,
Holding you in her cold green camera shutter eyes
Whose irises are segmented, like fine sections of a fruit.
She runs a manicured hand across the hard surface
Of her Vivienne Westwood snakeskin bag.
Her flesh is so soft,
It will split like a peach skin,
You know the fine spray that shoots out from the fruit
On a hot summer's day
As you run the paring knife along the contour
Of the curved peel,
All those fine hairs standing to attention,
And the others, their wounds cloaked in Versace,
They think they're playing the game.
Welcome to my world,
Only I know the rules.

2

He worked with blood, but the mirror was clean. His hand was still as it held the image. The camera zoomed in on the open window and captured her as she stood in violent twilight. Alone, exposed. He could smell her. The perfume of money rose from her skin. The shutter whirred in the still black garden.

There was not even the rustle of leaves as he captured her. The camera panned in closer as she shed her Damaris lingerie, a show for him. She was only a shadow in her world. Yet he would fetch from her the thing he craved, he would redesign her. He had her on film, her flesh could wait.

The Maserati gleamed in the parking lot, a boastful flash of burnished metal.

Leaving his office after a good day, Larry Fornalski opened the door to his glistening car and checked if he was being watched. You could say watching was a big part of his life. He was usually the one in the spectator's seat, but he liked to be seen with his Quattroporte S, his pride and joy.

The Maserati's looks aroused him with their assertive

poise and the hint of potential beneath the bonnet. He paused to admire his reflection in the polished Blu Nettuno metal. Feeling like a star in his own firmament, he ran his hand across his smooth bronzed jaw, lost in the mirror of his car.

In the lustre of the Blue Lacque wood trimming Larry caught a shadow moving at speed in the deserted lot. There was a noise like a shard of glass cracking beneath a leather sole on stone. He thought it was the night porter and looked around for him. But he had no point of reference for what he saw. It evoked a strange grimace, a final look in conflict on an unlined perfectly assured face. His expression was almost a pure piece of pantomime, as his death entered him. Hand on the roof of his redundant car, Larry fetched a choked scream from his throat.

The CCTV caught everything except the killer's face. A metre of blood shot outward from Larry's severed throat. He turned his head, his neck ejaculating onto the wall, and he toppled forward, his fingers streaming with blood.

The following morning Chief Inspector Jackson Flare and Inspector Mandy Steele examined the quarantined scene. Even behind his protective mask Flare's face looked weathered, as if life had corroded his skin. He held the right side of it away from Steele when he spoke to her. It was a habit he'd adopted for so long it gave him a surreptitious look.

'The killer escaped the camera', he said.

'He got in and out without being filmed, so he might work here', Steele said.

Flare looked at her out of the corner of his ice blue eyes. She never pitied him for his deformity. Whenever he caught a whiff of that his most vicious side surfaced like a criminal inside him.

'He knew what area the CCTV covers and how to avoid it', he said. 'All we can see is a tall figure in baggy clothes, he's wearing a hood of some description, and he's got his back to us.'

Steele stood several heads below Flare and as she looked up at him her dark eyes met his with fire and defiance. A strand of blonde hair peeped out of her head covering, irritating her. She liked it pulled back against her scalp, so that it stretched her skin.

'Could be a woman', she said.

'So we've got the victim at the extreme edge of the camera's range, the killer standing outside it. That's incredibly precise. It shows a technical mind. No car entering or leaving.'

'He was probably parked outside, there's a back lane he could have used which would have escaped detection.'

'We need some forensics.'

'Where's Maurice Ray when you want him?'

'Crime scene examiners hold things up. What is it with you and Maurice anyway?', Flare said.

'Me and Maurice?'

'You don't like gays or something?'

'He doesn't interest me', Steele said.

Just then the officer standing guard let Maurice Ray through.

'Morning Chief Inspector Flare', he said, and set about his job.

Steele stared at his back for a few minutes before walking over to him.

'Can you ID him?', she said.

'You in a hurry to leave?'

She folded her arms and waited as he lifted a wallet out of the victim's coat.

'His name's Larry Fornalski.'

'It seems Mr. Fornalski had enemies', Flare said. 'I know the name, he was in the papers the other day, a successful businessman. They always piss someone off on their way to the top. He's left the papers a gift, another piece of meat the press can sink their fangs into. We need to find out as much as we can about him.'

'I'll start digging back at the office', Steele said.

'Make the spade good and sharp.'

Steele looked down at the mutilated corpse and saw pornographic images. The faces of men she hated raced through her mind in a private reel of film. She turned her attention to Flare, who stood with his hands deep in his pockets looking at the severed neck with no trace of feeling.

'That's some weapon he used', he said, 'his head's almost hanging off.'

He left the scene and removed his mask, then walked

to the black unmarked Volvo V70. He took off his shoe covers and lit a Players, and sat there smoking with his foot astride the half-open door, his patent leather shoes a tawdry glow in the streetlight that failed to recognise day. The burning end of his cigarette moved like a ghostly wand in their polished surface.

Steele remained standing over Ray until he snapped off his gloves in irritation and walked outside. She followed him to the Volvo.

'I think I'll join you Chief Inspector Flare', Ray said, removing his mask.

Steele watched as he lit a More menthol. He was an extremely handsome man, with even features, clear tanned skin and an athletic build. He dragged deeply and moved the cigarette dramatically as he held it to his side, his wrist arched. He looked at Steele, then lowered his eyes and smoked in silence.

Steele kept her eyes on him, waiting for Flare to finish, trying to clear the stench of nicotine from her lungs, bracing herself for another day. She thought how suited Maurice Ray was to Mores, a woman's smoke, as if he had to make a statement about his sexuality. She tensed her muscles in the silence. She wanted to go back to the station, to dig into Larry Fornalski's past, to find out what secrets lay buried behind his murder. As she ran her eyes down Ray's body he looked up. Then he trod on the burning stub and said, 'I'll go and finish off'.

Flare stood and crushed the butt end of his cigarette on the side of a bin before flicking it in as Steele took off her mask and shoe coverings. She was an attractive woman with hard lines around her eyes.

Flare got in and started the engine. As Steele sat down she stole a glance at the other side of his face, its ravaged flesh, thinking it was like a foul disguise he was inviting her to remove.

Her skin crawled every time his hand brushed her knee when he changed gears.

She felt beyond his wound there lay some other world he was tempting her to enter.

3

In her drab pebble dashed house in Ealing, Gertrude Miller donned her pristine white gloves. She pushed them deep between her fingers, so there was no spare material, then smoothed out the cotton and held them up to the 100 watt bulb.

Gertrude was a tall woman with a full figure. She had a full sensuous mouth that was at odds with her austere face. It made her look as if she'd stolen someone else's lips. She wore no makeup and had a stern matronly look.

She walked over to the mantelpiece and ran her index finger along its edge, holding it up to the light when she'd finished. She did the same to the tops of the wardrobes, the kitchen appliances, the bookcases and the backs of the chairs, proceeding through the house room by room in an orderly manner, aware only of the slow ticking of the grandfather clock in the darkened hallway. When she'd finished she inspected her gloves. There was the tiniest residue of dust on one finger. Gertrude pulled them off and placed them in the washing machine, putting it on a boil wash. She watched them spin around in the soapy water on their own for a while before fetching the bees wax and polishing the clock. She looked at the time. Her children would be home any minute and she hadn't put the things out for their tea yet. They arrived just as she put the hot water in the pot.

'Mary, take off your shoes', she said.

Her daughter, thin and white as talcum powder, removed them standing on one foot before she left the mat, fully aware of the wrath her mother could unleash if she got any dirt on the carpet.

Maxwell, small and anxious, waited at the door while his sister preformed this ritual and then did the same, saying nothing and remaining silent throughout tea. When they were finished they went upstairs to do their homework. They never had to be told.

In the next room Gertrude tidied her hair, making sure no loose strands hung down. She always wore it scraped back, hiding its fullness beneath a harsh regime. As she moved away from the mirror she spotted a grey hair. It was hiding at the side and she neatly plucked it. There was the faint smell of meths in the austere bedroom, the product of her favoured method of cleaning mirrors.

She went downstairs to prepare supper. Ben would be back soon and hungry. She plumped the cushions in the living room and checked the street for any signs of him.

Behind the bubbling vegetables the frozen family portrait stared out at the vacant hallway.

Martha Fornalski sat in her rambling Holland Park house surrounded by Chihuahuas and clutching a tissue, a habit Flare found particularly disconcerting. She'd rolled it into a ball and he kept eyeing the mascara stain that edged its white circumference. From time to time she dabbed her swollen eyes.

Steele knew Versace and La Croix when she saw them and she stopped her brain's quick reckoning of how much money Martha was wearing. She was an attractive woman and Steele estimated she must have her share of interested men. Her dark hair lay gleaming on her shoulders and her full figure made itself known beneath her expensive clothes.

'What a day', Martha said, looking outside as the rain hammered the windows. 'I saw you walking around out there in all that mud before you rang.'

'Can you tell us about Mr. Fornalski?', Flare said.

'Larry was such a perfect husband. I mean, perfect. Worked hard, loved his kids. They're devastated. Who would do this?'

She laid her hands on her lap and looked at them both, her burgundy nails catching the overhead lights.

Flare avoided eye contact.

'We're trying to find that out, Mrs. Fornalski.'

The quiet ticking of the Ormolu clock was disturbed as the maid came in with a tray of tea and set it down on the table. Flare eyed the fussy porcelain with discomfort. He turned the disfigured side of his face away from Martha Fornalski as Steele poured two cups and passed him one. He took a sip and broke off a piece of short bread. Several large crumbs fell on the immaculate Persian rug and Flare ran the edge of his muddy shoe into it.

'I know it's hard for you to talk right now, Madam', Steele said, 'but are you aware of your husband having any enemies?'

'Larry? No.'

'I mean, someone at work or in business who may have felt slighted by him, however small, you just don't know.'

'No one!'

'Did Larry ever mention any one?'

'Everyone loved him. Work colleagues, friends. Larry never made enemies. He was one of the nicest easy going guys in the world. One in a million.'

Flare put his cup down, clattering the saucer. One of the Chihuahuas yapped at him and he stared at it in irritation.

Martha Fornalski looked over at Flare and allowed her gaze to drift, taking in the mark, her eyes watering, thinking of wounds, wanting to know how injured her husband was, not daring to ask.

'Do you think your husband told you everything?', Flare said.

'What sort of question is that?'

'Successful men have all sorts of nasty habits.'

'Nasty?'

'Did he have a mistress?'

'Now hold on a minute.'

Steele shot a glance at Flare.

'We're only trying to do our job, Madam', she said.

'Well, let us know if you think of anything', Flare

said, standing up. 'You never know. Sometimes families remember things after a while. Don't worry if it seems trivial, just ring. It might help us catch this man.'

He placed his card on the table.

As they followed Martha to the door the buckle of Flare's raincoat hit one of the Chihuahuas in the eye, prompting a howl.

They stepped out into the curtain of rain and sat in the car for a few minutes. Flare looked up at the immaculate Queen Anne brickwork, the ornate garden.

'How much do you think it's worth?', he said.

'Ten.'

'Ever think you're in the wrong job?'

'Never.'

'Buy the stuff about the nicest guy in the world?'

'She's his wife.'

'Nobody disliked him?'

'Someone did.'

'Steele people are scum.'

As they drove away, Ben Miller walked past the parade of dull houses marooned in their quiet suburban misery, put his key in the door, entered the hallway, and took off his shoes, balancing on one foot until he'd cleared the mat. He stood at six foot four and towered over his wife, who reached a cheek up into the air for him to kiss. When he'd done so, he moved his featureless face away from her.

'Good day, dear?', she said.

'Just fine.'

His voice was low and expressionless, as if he was speaking in the aftermath of some spent trauma.

'We've hotpot for supper, would you like a drink?'

'Please.'

Gertrude poured him a gin and tonic and held the glass to her ear, listening to the pleasant fizz, then fetched a clean tea towel and wiped the fine drops of water from her ear. She took Ben's slippers through to him in the living room, knelt and put them on him, then left him to read The Guardian while she called Mary and Maxwell for supper. Ben sat there raising the glass periodically to his thin lips, his white and shapeless hands turning the pages of the newspaper.

Gertrude seated the children, served the hotpot, and called him. The kitchen seemed too small for him as he entered, and he sat with difficulty on the chair, which looked like a child's seat beneath his frame. From time to time Gertrude glanced at him as he ate.

'Good, dear?'

'Very', he said, chewing slowly, with mechanical precision and without sound before swallowing, his massive Adam's apple rising and falling in the thick flesh of his neck like a buoy on water.

Afterwards Mary and Maxwell went upstairs and Gertrude and Ben sat in the living room. The folded newspaper lay at his side, the earmarked page with an article about abortions staring up at him. He watched the news, from time to time turning up the volume to drown out the incessant clicking of Gertrude's knitting needles. Their evening scrolled by like a meaningless script.

As they retired to bed in their quiet orderly manner Brian Samson left work. He'd set up his own hedge fund a few years ago and it was thriving. He'd made two mill on the markets that day and felt that deep warm glow of profit spreading across him like a hot bath. A Chateau D'Yquem seemed in order, but he needed something else since he'd been tasting blood all day, and he drove to see one of his favourite prostitutes in St James's on the way back to his Mayfair house where his wife Mirabelle was waiting. She'd drunk her way through two bottles of Montrachet and was now talking to Samantha DeLonge on the phone.

'Late again, what can I do? He was meant to be taking me out to dinner', she said, checking her manicure.

'He's always been a hard worker', Samantha said.

'Yes but this is ridiculous, who works this late?'

'A lot of guys. I know you didn't come from that background, but a lot of them do it, they expect their wives to tag along. Enjoy it. You got the lifestyle you wanted, why not take a lover?'

'That's the problem.'

'What?'

'That's what I think Brian's doing.'

'Brian screwing around? Why do you say that?'

'Something about the way he is with me.'

'Like what?'

'I don't know, like he doesn't want me anymore.'

'You know honey, when you're married you need to spice it up a little.'

'You mean kinky?'

'I mean lingerie, I mean make him want you, I mean don't always wait for him.'

'Make him want me', she said, her voice fading with indecision as the wine took hold.

'Honey, one night Paul got in from work, I was going through what you are and he found me in the kitchen making his dinner. I was all dressed up.'

'I cook for Brian all the time.'

'You know what I was wearing? Suspenders.'

'I wore suspenders two nights in a row and Brian never even made a pass.'

'No. I was wearing suspenders.'

'And nothing else?'

'You got it. So Paul walks in, smells dinner, then comes through to the kitchen, looks down at my arse and grabs me right there and then.'

'I'd have to be drunk.'

'So drink. I tell you, dinner got ruined, but some-thing else got cooked all right.'

From the outside, the house looked like another wealthy home, or even an office in St James's. But upstairs behind the window, Brian Samson was getting dressed. A tanned blonde with the figure of a model and a top range boob job was wriggling her naked hips into a Gucci python skirt. Brian Samson cast an admiring glance in her direction as she slipped on her sheer tiger print blouse.

'I like that', he said.

'The outfit?'

'The fact you never wear a bra.'

'Modesty doesn't become me.'

'Good night Simone', he said.

'See you soon.'

She showed him to the door and put the money away.

In the deserted streets below, Brian Samson drove home to a darkened house.

4

So simple, really
Run the knife across their well fed throats,
Watch the crimson blood bead there, lustrous in the light.
Surprising how much blood the bloodless have.
I favour the Vespula for its chromium stainless steel
blade,
It's tempered to Rockwell C58, hollow ground and mirror
polished
So you can watch their little faces fill with fear.
The handle is black Australian Nephrite Jade gemstone,
Reflective as polished chrome.
It has deep finger grooves and canted quillons,
It is perfect slashing equipoise
With razor-keen single bevel cutting edges.
I see it as a key for they close their doors on us.
I am the unlocker.
You can hide in corners, small cracks in the walls you
inhabit forever and a day
Well, I've got a thing or two to show them.

The following morning as Flare and Steele made their way to the station, Gertrude Miller hurried her children along, watchful that Ben was attended to.

'Mary, make sure you take everything, Maxwell, have you finished your breakfast without spilling any?'

Her questions were met with perfunctory grunts and soon they'd left.

Ben was standing in his underpants when Gertrude went upstairs to see if he needed anything.

'Benjamin? Oh, apologies.'

'It's all right', he said, 'come in. I think I'll just change these.'

She turned her back.

'Do you think I've put on weight?'

'I can't see from here.'

'Well, turn around.'

He was an imposing figure and he dwarfed the room as Gertrude kept her eyes fixed firmly on the far wall. In the mirror his naked form watched her. He turned and got dressed.

'That's better', she said.

'Why don't you want me?'

'Want you?'

'Yes. Sexually.'

'Why Benjamin, what's got into you? We have two beautiful children.'

'I know we have two children, how do you think they got here?'

'My, where does all this dust come from?', she said.

She was downstairs scouring saucepans when she heard the front door slam.

It seemed Larry Fornalski's wife was telling the truth.

'He was a genuinely popular guy who got on with just about everyone', Steele said. 'Colleagues described him as helpful and easy going and his friends are distressed at the news. There's no motive in his immediate circle. '

'Then we've got a problem', Flare said.

'Sure we've got a problem, a man's been killed and we've got no leads.'

Flare scraped the stubble on his chin with his nicotine stained fingernails.

'It could be a hit. Find out if he owed money, if behind the facade of a happily married man, Larry Fornalski was into gambling.'

Steele went outside to fetch a coffee before the long drudge through the data that she felt would eventually lead nowhere. In the corridor she ran into DI Vic Jones.

'Heard you got a new case Mandy.'

'Yes Vic, a pretty gruesome killing.'

'How's the old bastard taking it?'

She turned her face upwards, measuring him, her olive skin pale with stress.

'Oh, you know.'

She pressed for a black and watched the steam rise. Vic leaned against the machine, his wiry muscled frame casting a shadow that stretched past her along the corridor.

'That means he's making your life hell, the offer still stands.'

'I appreciate that, and I'm tempted, but.'

'Sticking with him?'

'Yes.'

'You serious?'

She looked into his cold eyes and held his gaze.

'He's a good detective.'

'He catches them, but his methods.'

'Vic, I've got to get on.'

'The only way you'll get on in the modern Met is to change your career path, get away from Flare, he'll bring you down, he belongs in the dark ages.'

'Right now, he's my partner.'

'He doesn't like anyone.'

'I didn't join the Met for a popularity contest.'

'I respect your determination.'

'I'll think about it Vic.'

'And all that shit with his face. You know how it happened? He was working someone over, I mean the governor said Flare could have been up for torture.'

'I'm not interested.'

'Harlan White is a real crim, probably deserved it, but that's not what we do.'

'Not anymore.'

He leaned into her, measuring her response.

'You do know, don't you?'

She raised a hand.

'Vic-'.

'He had a flame gun, he was burning his genitals. White turned it on Flare.'

She looked over his shoulder and he caught the flicker in her eye.

'Press white for me', Flare said. 'Oh and Vic, I think you've got genitals on the brain, leave my partner alone, there are plenty of whores out there for you to screw with.'

'Good morning to you too.'

'Is it, what's good about it? Like I said, give my compliments to your wife.'

Flare reached across him, took the coffee and walked away, followed by Steele.

A burnished sun burned bright in the sick London skyline as they toiled in darkness.

It sent shadows dancing across the Westway as Razor edged his white Lamborghini Gallardo past the hundred mark. The drivers he passed in a blur could just make out the flowing blonde hair in the passenger seat.

Anne Lacey watched the roads flash by.

'This is fucking great!', she said, unheard over the engine's dark noise.

Razor was never seen with anyone other than a model. His friends joked about Razor's Catwalk Pussy Parade. He'd made a fortune on the LA music scene and as he took Anne back to his house in Marylebone, he stopped at some lights.

The guys in the next car eyed her as she applied her

lipstick in the mirror. They rolled down their window to get a better look and from their radio Razor could hear one of his hits. He ran his hand through his golden mane.

'The system's a bitch' played loud and clear down Marylebone high street as he got ready for a quick session before the recording studio.

The digging was not as dull as Steele had expected. Larry Fornalski's bank statements were a dream.

Steele couldn't believe her eyes and resentfully pushed away the thought of her own financial position as an Inspector. She recalled the days when the title alone would have meant the world to her and now as she scrolled through the fiscal clout of this other world, she felt small and used, as if she'd sold herself some cheap con.

There were no anomalies in Fornalski's recent financial transactions. She went further back. There wasn't even the indication of the casual use of an expensive hooker.

He spent as a man in his position would, but it was all accounted for and nothing indicated he owed money to anybody.

'One thing's for sure', she said to Flare, 'Fornalski wasn't into gambling.'

That evening Martin Gould took the shortcut through

the passageway at the rear of his offices. It was a hot day and the heat lingered in the London air. He loosened his collar. He was a tall man who moved with that caution of added weight. He'd had a profitable afternoon and all he wanted was to get home, shower and take his wife out to dinner.

As he entered the relative darkness of the alley he thought about the deals he'd pulled off.

There was a lot of money heading his way. A lot.

The alley curved at the middle, losing light. The tall buildings towered overhead and he thought about traffic, picking the quickest route home. He kicked a can, which rolled noisily away from him. He slowed down, adjusting to the lack of light, and heard a noise behind him.

As he turned he felt something wet on his face, then a sharp pain. The taste of blood in his mouth. He could feel something entering him and warmth dripping from his body. He was amazed at the noise his own blood made.

MIRROR MAN

5

While you sleep I corrupt your faith,
While you dream I soil your wives.

There was one man Flare respected, a rarity in itself. That man was Frank Norris. He'd worked with him on many murders over the years. Norris always gave Flare what he wanted fast, there was no spare meat on their conversations, which was just the way Flare liked it. As he made his way down to the pathology lab with Steele, Flare said, 'I've got a feeling this is going to be a long case.'

'Why do you say that?'

He waited for the lift to start its descent into the dark bowels of the station.

'This killer's too careful. No evidence on camera, no sighting of his car. He knows what he's doing.'

In the lab Frank Norris was hunched over his work station, writing notes. His hair hung loosely in a pony tail over his collar and he turned his masked face to theirs. Stubble stuck out from the top and his eyes looked black and burnt out.

'Good afternoon, Detectives', he said, 'why is it that

the bloody paperwork seems to get more every day?'

'Don't even ask', Flare said.

'Do the politicians know what our jobs entail?'

'I don't think the politicians know anything.'

'Well', he said, pulling the sheet back on Larry Fornalski's corpse, 'he was killed with a sharp knife. An extremely sharp knife. One usually used to gut fish.'

'Easily available?'

'I'd say you could buy it at most good angling shops, Jackson. Not that I think you're looking for a keen fisherman.'

'You got something juicy for us?'

He walked over to a work bench and picked up a petri dish, which he handed to Flare.

'What the hell is that?'

'Mr. Fornalski's Adam's apple. His throat was so gashed you wouldn't have noticed it missing, but our killer removed it and forced him to eat it.'

'To eat it?'

'He would have been alive still, just about, and probably drifting in and out of consciousness, but the killer rammed it down his throat as a last offering.'

'Ever come across this before Frank?'

'Not this. I've seen cannibalism and the ritual removal of organs, trophy keeping by killers. And there's one other curious thing.' Norris turned Fornalski's head, and pulled down his ear. 'The killer has cut the letter B into his skin. I'd say he used a scalpel and he's been very precise in shaping the letter.'

Outside in the corridor Flare noticed Steele looking green.

'You'll get used to it.'

Alone in his loft conversion, surrounded by Giotto prints, he made ready. Dressed from head to foot in black velvet, he cut an imposing figure as he strode across the floor, muscular and choreographed in his movements.

The place was immaculate. It was show room. Auction catalogues lay in neat piles on various antique tables. The huge windows looked out at the towering landscape of London below, the Thames stretching like a coiled snake into the polluted distance where a bleeding sun sank without promise into its foul waters. Boats bobbed by without noise and a few gulls squabbled in the grey air.

A candle guttered at the window as he moved towards his corrupted faith, hung there like a parody of the mass. He stopped before this still and waxen Christ, such as is seen in the churches of the Mediterranean, and looking up at the tortured body he began to desecrate it. He took a switchblade from his pocket and spitting on it like a back alley mugger he ran the saliva along the edge of the blade with his thumb. Then he pierced him. His face was contorted with pleasure and his neck twitched.

Licking his lips he stared into Christ's eyes and stabbed him in his groin, cutting the statue, so that shards and fragments fell to the spotless floor. He removed the head and kicked it across the open room with only the untenanted sky as witness to his delirium.

Finally he lay twitching at the statue's feet, his body convulsing. He lay there with his hand against his crutch, staring wildly up at nothingness until he was still again.

6

Sick little people in their sick little world
I don't know who hates them more, me or Jackson Flare.

Razor looked at her as she lay sleeping. He liked them unconscious. He could observe so much about them, things they gave away and hid during the day.

Sunrises drifted across his frozen coke numb mind, etchings of things he wanted to do to his Pussy Parade. Her flesh was like honey and he ran a cold finger along her inner thigh, feeling the fine hairs against his skin. She stirred in her velvet sleep.

She was tanned and beautiful and didn't ask any questions. Her stomach and breasts rose and fell with her breath on his black silk sheets. They'd been lying there for hours and he wanted to cut another track at his studio.

He went into the bathroom and shut the door. He sliced himself some lines and wiped away the white mark on his nose and headed down to his car. A cop crossed the street and a wave of paranoia passed across him like a current. A trickle of sweat ran down his face. He checked himself in the mirror. Some kids walked by laughing and he jumped. He'd finish his session and go back for some more. She'd be there. So would the coke. Ignoring the speed cameras, he drove to the studio as fast as he could.

As the moon hung like a soiled light bulb in the dirty London skies, Gertrude Miller finished polishing the glasses. Ben sat reclining in his easy chair watching the news, Mary and Maxwell were in bed, as she pulled on her white gloves to do a quick dust check. She found nothing, not a single speck, and she felt a gnawing emptiness inside her. In the living room Ben was glued to the TV screen. The police were arresting some men who held their faces down, away from the camera. She listened to the newscaster.

'Some of these women have been forced into prostitution, they have no choice. Brought here as asylum seekers they fall prey to a vicious black market that leaves them trapped in a sickening trade that is escalating on a daily basis. This is just the beginning of a massive police crackdown on what is a worrying problem.'

She reached across Ben, took the remote control and switched the TV off.

'I was watching that.'

'Do you want to go to bed?'

'Oh, you didn't like the subject matter. Sex.'

'Come on.'

She led him upstairs to the bedroom, where he put the light on.

'No. Dark', she said.

He obliged and removed his clothes and stood there waiting.

Soon he mounted her in his lumbering bovine manner and she lay immobile until he was finished when she went into the bathroom to wash.

She squatted on the bidet and ran her plump index finger inside herself, scooping out Ben's semen. She flicked the thick globules onto the immaculate bleached porcelain, where they hung until the jet removed them.

7

'They'll have to hose this alley down when we're finished', Flare said.

He and Steele were looking over Maurice Ray's shoulder at the mutilated body of Martin Gould and they both knew they were staring down the barrel of a serial killer's gun.

'The cut's different this time', Ray said.

Flare knelt and looked at the wound. It ran several inches vertically down his neck, progressing through his blood soaked shirt collar.

'He's sliced him right to his heart', Ray said. 'The clothes are torn and clinging to the wound, the blood's congealed and holding them in place.'

'The killer must have been waiting for him', Flare said. 'He's handpicking his victims.'

'Serial territory', Steele said.

Martin Gould had turned the alley red and he lay there like some ritual offering to the darkness.

The alley was littered with food wrappers, coffee cups, and crushed drink cans. A copy of Hustler lay open a few feet from his body. Steele stared down at the image of a naked woman staring into the camera with legs parted, her knees on her chest.

'Why does pornography always make genitals look like wounds?', she said.

They left Maurice Ray taking pictures and returned to the station. Later that day they drove round to see his wife Sandra.

The door to her imposing Hampstead home was so immaculate that as they stood there they could see their own reflections in the black paint. Flare's wounded face looked like a scarcely beating heart in the burnished gloss.

An attractive brunette with not a hair out of place opened the door and stood there looking at them with an expression of surprise which quickly turned to horror as Flare took out his badge.

They followed her through to the drawing room, where she poured herself a glass of vintage Courvoisier cognac. As she sipped deeply from the tulip glass with perfect lips, Steele once again noticed the designer labels she was wearing and resented her model's figure beneath the Gucci and Ferretti. She looked like she'd stepped straight from a Glamour magazine.

'This is the second murder we've investigated in a week', Flare said. 'We're looking at the possibility that someone may be stalking and killing businessmen and we're working on the hypothesis that there's an explanation for this in their business dealings. I know this is hard for you, but you will be helping us and your husband if you can think of anyone he may have fallen out with or had a disagreement with recently.'

'Martin?'

'Did he have any enemies, Mrs. Gould?', Steele said.

'No.'

'Did he mention any disagreements at work?'

'I can't think of any.'

'Are you aware of anything out of the ordinary that may have happened to your husband in the past weeks?', Flare said.

'Nothing. He worked hard and when he wasn't at the office he was here.'

'With you.'

Sandra's eyes narrowed.

'With me.'

'Did he keep regular habits?', Flare said.

'Yes.'

'You never suspected your husband was hiding something from you?'

'No.'

Sandra Gould stared at Flare, her eyes brimming with tears.

Steele stood up.

'Well, keep thinking and if anything does occur to you, please let us know.'

Outside Flare looked at Steele.

'In future, you let me cut the interviews short.'

'She was in no fit state.'

'So we're seeing all these perfect husbands killed, what's that say?'

She looked at him with opaque eyes.

'Perfect husband? No such thing.'

They found out a few things about Martin Gould. A

partner with Slaughter and May, he'd worked on some of the hardest cases and won. In fact he'd never lost.

'This guy was *the* lawyer if you wanted one. He had the most meticulous briefs, and he could articulate an argument out of a tin can against carbonated drinks while sipping one', Flare said. 'And how he charged.'

'OK, so we've also got Larry Fornalski, successful businessman, made millions out of asset stripping, what's the connection?'

'Money.'

'More than that?'

'Gould could have pissed a lot of people off.'

'Wives both loved them', Steele said.

'Wives aren't the best judge, maybe these women got what they wanted.'

8

Razor was high. Too high for Anne's liking. She'd been here before with guys in the fashion world and she didn't like the spiral he was headed down.

'I like your eyes Anne', he said, 'they're green like no green ever seen, they look like little cameras staring at me. Whirr click. Do you think it's all the shots you've had taken on the catwalk?'

'Let's go out and eat', she said, pulling his hand away from the mirror.

'One more, sweetheart one more. Your mouth looks like it wants to bite something, fancy giving me a blowjob?'

A call came in on her i Phone. Razor drifted while she chatted to a friend. When she finished he was lying on the bed with a bottle of Chopin vodka unzipping his trousers.

'Come on, let's do it', he said.

'I'm meeting some of the girls.'

'Who is he?', Razor said, jumping up.

'No one, Razor, come with me.'

'You said you'd fuck me.'

'I don't like this.'

'You're gonna like this, you bitch!'

He threw her on the bed and started to tug at her bra. As one breast popped out she kneed him in the groin.

Just as she got to the door, she felt a hand on her leg and he pulled her to the ground where he started kicking her, digging the steel tips of his cowboy boots deep into her body. He didn't stop kicking her until she passed out. Razor slipped in some of Anne's blood. Her face was a livid colour as he went out and got pissed.

In her unlit bedroom Gertrude Miller stood at her tired windows looking nervously out at the grey street below. She hid behind the curtains and watched the man who loitered by some dustbins. He lit a cigarette and looked up. The burning end of the cigarette looked like a dying coal against his dirty grey hair, and the hand he held to his mouth was darkened even at a distance by the tattoo that stretched its way across it like a black tide.

She retreated into the room, pressing herself against the wooden cupboard, concealed there. She waited, holding her breath, as he walked slowly past her house and paused. She didn't notice the wet patch on her tweed dress until he disappeared at the end of the road. Finally when she emerged downstairs she began to prepare dinner before Ben returned.

In their rooms Mary and Maxwell toiled at homework, aware of the punishment their mother would inflict if they failed to finish. Downstairs steam rose and curtained the windows as the saucepan lid heaved and bubbled.

9

Flare felt the skin, the puckered flesh like a terrain of calluses against his fingertips. He moved his face one way, then the other, watching his twin selves. He often thought the unmarked side of his face was his cop's face. The other side was the man he'd be if he broke the law.

He turned the rusted tap, half expecting to see blood gush from it, and held his hands under the flow of water. The rage wouldn't settle and he started to punch the wall, cracking a tile. He steadied his face into a mask, freezing his feelings until he could walk outside and deal with his colleagues.

As he looked at himself in the mirror he saw his father standing against the wall. The reason he became a cop, the watcher in his brain. He was the reason he craved the absolution of legality like a needle in an itching vein. As if he could push criminality aside as easily as that. The old feeling was returning and he had to manoeuvre each muscle into place to be the man he was at work.

His own footfalls echoed in his head as he trod the empty corridor back to his office. He eyed his partner surreptitiously as she sat glued to her computer screen, a flicker of menace in his eyes. He noticed how soft the skin at the back of her neck was and swallowed hard, tasting bile.

Brian Samson finished his busy day at around eight and picked up the phone. Getting Mirabelle's voicemail was welcome, he didn't want conversation.

'Hi darling, it's me. Still tied up, should be back later.'

A healthy profit called for a healthy celebration and he drove to St James's.

After ringing the bell and waiting a few minutes he retreated into the street to look up at the window. No lights. Unusual for Simone, even if she was out.

He rang her private number, the one she gave only to her most exclusive clients, and heard the message she left that morning.

'Hi, I'm away for a few days holiday, but I'll be back even more tanned and ready for you, so be a good boy and leave a message and I'll give you a massage.'

He hung up, irritated at the invasive presence of a life she led outside his contracting of her services.

Driving home he rummaged in his briefcase. A magazine ad had caught his eye earlier, and he found it at some traffic lights.

'Buxom lady can help businessmen relax. Exclusive and professional services.'

He folded the page. He returned to an empty house and a sense of irritation that even a bottle of Pauillac wouldn't shift.

When Mirabelle returned, his tired attempts to drag her to bed ended with a fumble and a slap. She wasn't used to being treated like this and he found himself waking in the spare room in the small hours.

Filthy deeds and filthy acts,
All they want is to relax.

THE WHIPMASTER

10

Reflections linger
In chrome,
Still water,
Designer handbags,
Camera lenses.
Yet the image is not the same in reflection
It is altered by the mirror
As you are replicated so you are absorbed.
Have you ever paused to consider
As the pictures of you
Dance across screens,
Shop windows,
Bright metals,
Nail polish,
How altered you are?
The mirror makes identity.

The house was dark. Martha Fornalski sat, mind wandering, her cold hand clutching the doctor's prescription for Valium. She nodded to herself.

'They're all in it together', she said, standing and turning on a lamp.

She stood before a Silver Rocco mirror and smoothed her dress. She liked to see her firm body outlined against a silver frame. It made her feel timeless and expensive.

'I'll do, but then I always did', she said, hearing her voice echo in the room.

She crumpled the prescription, threw it into the bin, and turned to look at one of the photos of Larry that lined the wall. He was smiling after one of his big deals. His teeth shone like diamonds. She remembered the day well. His drunkenness and the demanding sex. Her internal pain hadn't stopped for days afterwards. She turned the picture round, catching a flash of anger on her face in the polished glass, and proceeded to walk from room to isolated room. She pulled a bottle of Pouilly Fuisse out of the fridge. The pop of the cork conjured the noise of the bathroom door flying open as Larry kicked it off its hinges.

The scene was alive again, a piece of living torture she couldn't purge from her soul.

'You fucking bitch, showing yourself like that', Larry said, standing over her as she clutched the towel about her, water dripping from her calves.

She'd known a rage was coming, they were infrequent in the latter days of his life, a common experience at the beginning of their marriage, when she would frequently plan to leave him. But his money held her there like a hook set deep in a fish's gills.

'Larry, what are you talking about?', she said, knowing how weak this remonstration was.

'This.'

He pulled the towel from her and looked at her body with a mixture of disgust and desire as she wondered if all men hid their sexual needs.

'Have you lost your mind Larry?'

'Why do you keep shaving it?'

He grabbed her crutch and pushed her to the floor. She felt him enter her and flood her with hot angry semen as she traced the distant line of a crack on the bathroom ceiling.

Afterwards he got up and left, saying over his shoulder 'You're my wife, not some object on display for other men to watch. Next time you tell me when you shave.'

She lay there with his sperm running cold onto her thigh, thinking but that is what I am, his object of display, a living walking handbag he can carry around and stuff with all the things he doesn't want to hold, he enjoys men seeing me.

Now she sat drinking as nighttime fell, her eyes brimming with tears. From the street the house looked deserted, like some stranded ferry of misery.

Sandra Gould, by contrast, had every bulb burning in her huge rambling Hampstead mansion, the house she now owned, a fact she kept reminding herself of. She moved from one glass of vintage Courvoisier to another, which lay spread around at strategic points so that she could just reach out and grab one when she felt like it. She'd been pouring it all day and was talking to Lucinda Hereford on the phone.

'The police have been asking whether Martin had enemies', Sandra said.

'Everyone's got enemies, it's what business does.'

'My God, you should have seen the two freaks they sent round. One looked like an extra in a horror film, the other a porno reject.'

'We don't deal with the police.'

'The Chief Inspector is an unpleasant man, making insinuations. And his sidekick has whore written all over her, a little tart who probably doesn't own a single piece of designer clothing.

Martin got on with people, he didn't go out of his way to piss people off.'

'I know.'

'It was so violent, he didn't deserve that.'

They said their goodbyes and she hung up and went upstairs. In the empty bedroom she slowly unbuttoned her metallic Versace blouse. Then she slipped out of her Christian Lacroix skirt and stood by the lamp sipping from her glass, a voluptuous Damaris silhouette stencilled against the window. She didn't hear the rustle in the bushes, nor see his shadow accelerate across the well tended lawn at the back where he watched her move half naked in her private hell.

The whirr and click of the black S2 Leica camera shutter were appreciated only by the figure whose still hands held it as Sandra slipped out of her lingerie into the night.

11

The lens has her,
She will stay at optimal resolution
In eternal erotic zoom.
There is no vignetting in the frame that holds
Nubile Sandra.
I like her best in her bubble gum pink silk tulle
Pannetoni Bra and back Bow Knickers,
Her body is so familiar without them.

'They don't know, Max.'

'What did the police ever know, Paul?'

'You're right.'

'They're not part of what we are, they belong to a different world.'

The two men talking were Max Hereford and Paul DeLonge. They were sitting on a bench by the Italian pond in Hyde Park. Its surface looked like glass. They paused as a young woman talking on her mobile walked by. Although she was lost in conversation, they eyed her with suspicion until she was out of earshot, her reflection accompanying her along the still surface of the water.

'They're looking in all the wrong places', Max said.

'They'll never find out about us.'

Max looked at Paul and lit a Sobrani Royale cigarette. He inhaled deeply before releasing a plume of blue smoke that headed skywards.

'He did do some terrible things', he said.

'Yes, we know what he put Martha through.'

'Larry's marriage is private, it is not something the police have any right snooping into.'

'We keep them out.'

'I have an appointment', Max said, standing up.

'Watch the police intrusion and tell me if anything comes up.'

They clasped hands, the gold rings both wore on their middle fingers clanging against each other. They were a simple design of black Nephrite Jade bearing the letters GC set in the stone in Palatino.

Max walked away and Paul sat there like a statue, unseen and watchful, a living camera in the Park.

Anne Lacey left hospital with a broken mandible bone in her face, two cracked teeth and multiple bruising. She told the police she'd been attacked by an unknown assailant, preferring to press Razor for money. As soon as she got back to her flat in Kensington she left a message on his voicemail.

'Razor, Anne. I'd like the bill settled, call me.'

She stood staring at herself in the bathroom mirror, rage working its way through her body as she thought of all she wanted to do to him.

Two hours later Razor returned from a recording session. He heard her message, got ten grand out of the bank and hand delivered it. By the time he returned, there was another message from her.

'Got your parcel, Razor. Didn't you want to come up and see me? If you think this is the last you've heard of this, you've got another thing coming. I'm losing work you fucking coke head arsehole, do you know what a top model gets paid? Call me. If you know what's best for you.'

'It's his finger this time', Frank Norris said.

Flare and Steele were standing in the pathology lab as Norris went through his findings on Martin Gould.

'Lodged in his throat?', Flare said.

'Very deftly removed. The killer sliced it off, with the wedding ring still on it, eighteen carat gold and a fine diamond at the centre, tastefully done, if a man wears that sort of thing-'.

'Spare us the jewellery.'

'The point I'm making is that he could have picked any finger.'

'It's his marriage the killer's making a point about', Steele said.

'Exactly.'

Flare nodded.

'So he doesn't like happily married men.'

'It's more than that. His wedding ring was placed

on his middle finger, as you can see there's a tan line indicating a wider ring was worn there.'

'So where's the other ring?', Flare said.

'He put it on the severed ring finger.'

'And rammed it down his throat', Flare said.

He and Steele peered into the petri dish.

'What does that say on the ring?', she said.

'GC', Norris said.

Flare turned to him.

'What does that stand for?'

'That's your department, I'm just telling you what was done to him. And I can tell you the man you're looking for is very good with sharp instruments. He sliced his finger off as easily as a piece of chicken breast.'

'The man we're looking for', Flare said, thinking how far they were from even beginning to find him. 'Any letters on him?'

'Yes. Left ear the letter D.'

Flare and Steele looked at it.

'Neatly cut', Steele said.

'I think he's trying to tell you something', Norris said.

On their way back to the office Flare said to Steele, 'I'm calling in Don Harvard. He's a profiler and may just be able to help.'

12

Brian Samson was feeling extremely frustrated. Simone was still away and he hung up in annoyance at hearing her voicemail again. Mirabelle had organised a busy week of dinners which left him little time for anything else. Work was no good without play, and play was the thing he looked forward to most when he was pulling off a deal.

That afternoon he looked at Mirabelle as she got ready to go out to lunch. She was always immaculate, and her taste in clothes was, if expensive, discreet. She was attractive and desirable but, Brian thought, totally without sexual adventure. No danger and no dirt. Just a wife. But then that was why he married her. Everything in its place and a place for everything. There were other hookers.

Mirabelle put the finishing touches to her lipstick, puckering and pinching her lips between a tissue. She eyed Brian in the mirror. He was sprawled out on the bed and he caught her eye.

'Ready?', she said.

'Darling, I'm always ready for you.'

Martha Fornalski hurried from her house into her Mercedes. She was meeting Sandra Gould for lunch at Le Feu, and she felt raw, as if someone had peeled her skin away. Her Cartier sunglasses did little to hide her discomfort. She wanted to wear cheap clothes, like the mothers at the supermarkets, and hide behind brands that had no cachet. The enjoyment of being watched was gone from her, and she wondered if there were places she could go anonymously and blend into a crowd, lost among the little people she never knew.

Two cars behind her, a white van followed, the driver pulling back from time to time. When she got to the restaurant, he passed her, noting the dress she wore, a black chiffon Alberta Ferretti, stylish and most becoming a woman in grief. It complimented her figure and he was pleased. She didn't hear the whirr of the shutter as he took a picture.

Inside Sandra was waiting. Her Channel sunglasses lay on the table before her and she wore a Hermes scarf and black Versace dress. She and Martha lunched on salmon, sharing a bottle of Mouton-Rothschild.

'We're both widows now', Sandra said.

Martha nodded.

'Wealthy women.'

'So what do we do with our money now we're on our own?'

Martha paused, and prodded the food at the edge of her plate with her fork.

'Are we on our own? Our marriages were not like other peoples'.'

'Yes, we were our husbands' baubles, and they both enjoyed seeing how desired we were.'

'Wasn't that the thing we sought?'

'Of course. To be watched and beyond the touch of men who can't afford us.'

'Did you ever feel like a commodity?', Martha said.

'Every day.'

'That time Larry raped me it was all so clear I was just a piece of his property. He wanted me on display.'

'And yet he didn't. Only people like us would understand.'

'We inhabit a closed world.'

'With its distinct pleasures', Sandra said.

They settled the bill and brushed each others' cheeks with their lips before parting. Martha returned home while Sandra paid a visit to her safe deposit box in Knightsbridge. The manager greeted her by her first name and then left her alone.

She sat and went through the money. She calculated that with what Martin had left she could make some changes.

That afternoon she put her house on the market with Savills and placed a deposit on a property in Barbados. She then toured the designer shops in London, returning with more bags than she could carry.

13

Don Harvard turned up at the station that afternoon. He strode into the office while Flare was mid-conversation with Steele. She turned to see an even featured well groomed man dressed in a pinstripe suit, a man who she might have thought attractive were it not for his fussy appearance. There was something too placed about him for her liking.

'Thanks for coming Don', Flare said. 'This is DI Steele.'

'Pleased to meet you.'

'Likewise.'

'You got my email?', Flare said.

'I did. It's been a hectic day, but I'll tell you what I can gather so far. This man is very neat and observational. He's a watcher. He knows exactly what he is going to do beforehand.'

'Motive?', Flare said.

'Too early to say yet, but I wouldn't be surprised if this is a revenge killing.'

'Why do you say that?'

'Because there's a very precise element to the way he's mutilated these two men, and that indicates foreknowledge of the victim.'

'How well do you think he knew them?', Steele said.

'Hard to say, but he wanted to inflict something specific on them.'

'And the letters?'

'Did you ever read Franz Kafka's story In The Penal Colony?'

'I carry it around in my back pocket', Flare said.

'Most droll. In it prisoners' sentences are inscribed on their skins as part of an execution process.'

'What does this tell us about the killer?'

'To him the victims are papyrus, he's etching his truth into them, owning their flesh and ruining it at the same time. I'd say it's sexual. He's getting aroused by killing them in this way, he's penetrating them first with his truth.'

14

Once Mary and Maxwell had gone to school, Gertrude Miller inspected the house and found everything to her satisfaction. As she sat down to do some knitting a figure passed by the window, his shadow leaning on the far wall.

She rose from her chair and stood at the side of the lace curtain, looking out through the chink. A man with black hair was vanishing at the street's end. She relaxed. The man who was following her hadn't been back. She thought she saw him in the supermarket the other day, but when she turned, the hair was wrong, a different grey.

She went upstairs to a cupboard in the hall. Reaching into her pocket she extracted a small key which she used to open the padlock. She was always blaming Mary and Maxwell for playing with her household supplies and had locked them away for years. She reached inside for a second key and then went into the bedroom to change.

Removing her overall and stiff white blouse, she slipped out of the grey skirt and emerged a while later wearing a tight black dress that was open at the top and showed the lace edge of her bra. She slipped a pair of shoes into a bag and put on an overcoat.

Don Harvard looked in detail at Frank Norris's report, noting the differences between the cutting directions the killer used on the two victims. He held the photos to the light, running his eyes down the incisions, acknowledging the neat work. He examined the letters found on both victims, scanning them into his computer and putting them into various search engines. Then he rang Flare.

'I knew this guy was an inscriber', he said, 'but it's more specific than I realised.'

'The letters?'

'Yes.'

'What have you got?'

'The D is the shape of the D of Damaris, the B of Bordelle.'

'And they are?'

'Expensive brands of lingerie.'

'What is he saying?'

'The key is in branding, in the sense of designer goods and branding his victims. The motive is sexual.'

15

He emerged through a doorway to the left wearing a long flowing black velvet coat and walked over the broken idol. Gathering the pieces, he placed them in the rubbish and then went into the next room from which he removed another Christ. He placed this against the window. Whips of various sizes were laid out on a table. Picking up a twelve inch bullwhip and lovingly gripping the handle, he began to strike the statue. The sounds were sharp and resonant in the static room.

He walked up to the statue and held his face against it, watched by the gentle tortured eyes. Then he began his strange defilement with his body tensed and alert, his face twitching in ecstasy. He pushed his crutch forward and curled the whip against the still air, slicing it through empty space, pausing to consider the sound it made. Flakes of paint fell like snow to the floor. He put the bullwhip on the table and picked up a blacksnake whip, caressing the rawhide handle, fingering the rounded end, and continued hitting Christ.

He paraded his torture in a show of prowess. He braced himself against the hanging body.

He laid his hand on his groin. He erased its image from his mind.

'I like women who cooperate', Brian Samson said.

He looked at her, the long auburn hair cascading down her shoulders, the ripples merging with her cleavage. He felt appreciative. He'd found another one.

'I always cooperate', she said, coming closer and loosening his tie, 'now what do you want me to do?'

Brian reached out and squeezed one of her ample breasts, running his thumb across the outline of her nipple beneath the bra. Her skin was white and he thought of tanned toned Simone, and how she catered to his desires.

'What brand is it?', he said.

'La Senza. It's a Bon Bon Frill.'

'Not the most upmarket.'

'I think I know what you want', she said, and gently pushed him onto the bed where she undid his trousers. Then she got undressed and pulled down his pants.

'Now, what do you want me to do with it?', she said, picking up his penis.

'There are a couple of things.'

He looked over at the money he'd laid on the table. He wanted satisfaction for his cash.

He noticed she kept her stilettos on and she followed the line of his eyes.

'Off?', she said.

'Sergio Rossi?'

'Mary Jane.'

'Isn't that the style of the shoe not the brand?'

'I don't know about brands, I know what you want though. Now on or off?'

'Off.'

He watched as she lifted up one foot and removed it. Then she raised her other foot and ran the heel across his crutch.

'Help me?'

He lifted it off and let it drop.

'You know I like the way you don't shave', he said, 'most women like you wax.'

'Why would I shave?', she said. 'I'm not a man, I always tidy my garden.'

He put his hand between her legs and ran his hand across the tuft of hair. She turned and he looked at her backside, the curves taut as she bent to fetch something from her bag.

He could hear a squeaking noise as she donned pink rubber gloves. He was about to speak when she laid her hand between his legs.

'You're going to like this' she said.

He looked at the ceiling.

'I've never had this done before.'

'You're a dirty boy, I'm going to clean your penis, but first I'm going to empty it.'

When she was finished he got dressed and watched her throw a robe over herself.

'I look forward to seeing you again, next time fucking you.'

'I work Mondays and Wednesdays', Gertrude said.

Brian Samson walked down the spoiled staircase to the street outside and drove out of Acton.

16

Don Harvard was going through his profile of the killer with Flare and Steele.

'So what's your take on these lingerie makes?', Flare said.

'Damaris is an exclusive brand.'

'Any psychological significance in it?'

'None that leaps out at me with Damaris, but with Bordelle there may be. Much of it is designer bondage, sophisticated to suit the tastes of women who may like doing something a little bit risqué in the bedroom.'

'So the killer is targeting people he sees as perverted?', Flare said.

'There's no perversion indicated with Damaris. The brands could mean all kind of things.'

After Don had left Flare said to Steele 'These brands mean anything to you?'

'Me? I'm a Marks and Spencer girl.'

He lit a cigarette, his stained hand like a glove against his face.

The bus pulled away and he walked slowly round the corner, past the shoppers and into the side street. When he came to the door he rang and entered as the buzzer sounded.

Then he climbed the staircase, his footsteps silent, as if he'd developed a habit of noiseless approach out of some native menace.

The peeling door opened and the face that greeted him was far from friendly, although it assumed the expression of professional charm, the lines altering quickly to their assumed positions, forced on them by years of habit and practice before the mirror.

'Thought you were away', he said, moving into the lurid hallway light, his dirty grey hair like a shock of stained wool.

'You know I don't work every day.'

He went through to the bedroom and started undressing.

As she went to fetch something he said 'That's why I went to your house.'

She paused, hand on the doorframe.

'What?'

'That's why I went to your house', he said, looking straight at her.

'You don't know where I live.'

'I followed you. I saw you looking at me out of the window.'

'You must be mistaken.'

'No. It was you.'

'Keith it can't have been.'

'It was you. Gertrude.'

'Why are you calling me that?'

'It's your name.'

'No, Keith.'

'You saw me at the window, you saw me and moved away, Gertrude.'

'Oh, I see, one of your fantasies. I'll be whoever you want me to be, now let me get my gloves on.'

She went into the kitchen where she opened a drawer. It contained only a few blunt knives and forks, some spoons and a pizza cutter. She could hear him calling to her.

When she returned he said 'I'm going to go back to your house to speak to that husband of yours, does he know what you do?'

'I'm not married.'

'Big bloke, isn't he? I bet he'd knock you about if he found out.'

'If you want me to be married, I'll be married.'

'It's not the first time I've been down your street.'

He was removing his trousers when Gertrude pulled the pizza cutter from her dress. She ran it under his double chin. It reminded her of cutting fat off the meat for supper and this intrusion of home life at the flat angered her. She forced the metal deeper into the side of his neck.

He looked at her with a slow grin of blood forming below his face, as if his laceration brought with it the dawning comprehension of a joke he'd laboured to understand for years, the beads forming slowly on the fresh cut and dripping down onto his chest.

Gertrude grabbed his filthy hair and pulled his head

back as he reached for her and she cut him again, this time producing a shower of blood. She watched as he sprayed the carpet and the walls and then fell to his side.

She turned off the intercom and began to clean the room. She spent hours scrubbing the blood from the fixtures, before removing the carpet. Then she returned for him, rolling him into the underlay and dragging him downstairs and into her waiting car. She drove into a deserted street and dumped the body. Then she returned home.

CAMERA OBSCURA

17

Harlan White was a pimp and a dealer who enjoyed torturing people. He'd maimed many of the prostitutes who worked for him once they were no longer useful. He never expected Flare. Not in a million years.

When he dodged two convictions thanks to his lawyer, Flare cornered him one day on a minor harassment charge. It was early on in Flare's career. He took him into an interview room where he extracted such a dark confession from him that Flare's superior was not sure which he was more shocked by: what White had done or what his own officer had done to him.

White had been carrying out abortions on his women and selling the babies on the black market. Since his abortionist's skills were close to butchery, the women became second rate commodities to him. He chained them up in his basement where he left them to starve, and charged low fees for pervs to go down and use them as they wished until they died.

Flare had initially intended to scare White. But then White burned him. When Flare got the flame gun back off him he held it so close to White's genitals he had none left.

Flare's superior officer covered it up. He was about to retire and didn't want to be involved in a lengthy inquiry.

The evening after Harvard's second visit to the station Flare sat at home and searched for White's movements on his computer. The latest case had evoked memories. The killer's inscriptions on his victims made Flare think of White. He felt branded and was unable to forget him every time he looked in the mirror.

Mandy was enjoying a night out with the girls, none of them police officers. She needed to taste the life she led away from work. The Vintner's Nose was a clean, sparkling bar in Kensington she liked. It was full of people she didn't understand, people far from who she was and that part of herself she detested.

She needed a break from police mentality and as she got drunker on Chardonnay she eyed the couples who came and went with a mixture of envy and resentment. Wealth and hope hung off them like swear words etched into their designer clothes.

Their lives, so neat on the surface, seemed to her to conceal a web of lies and little secrets. As Steele peered into the empty bottle she realised she was staring down the abyss at the constant potential for crime. How many of these seemingly innocuous people were hiding things she might arrest them for? Policing removed trust and its absence yielded strange desires.

She told herself she liked being single and that it secured her ability to judge as a detective, hardened as she was against the sentiments that ruled most people's lives. She could pick who she went out with and for how long and she wasn't in any rush to settle down.

Two women entered the pub with their partners and she read them as suckers, falling for their lies. Her old life hovered before her like some sick perpetrator she'd failed to arrest. She swigged back the dregs in her glass, waiting for the fraying of the image of who she was, of who she was trying not to be as a policewoman, and she knew deep inside she was hungering for a release and that hunger was growing while she failed to catch this killer who bore all the trademarks of a shadow from her dreams.

Casting only a single glance at her friends who stood at the bar, she stole out into the empty street. Her hands were shaking and she looked about her for criminals, vagrants, anyone who she could use to release her latent malice, seeing only a woman in a headscarf shuffle from a doorway.

She walked, her high heels clacking on the pavement that echoed with the hollowness of her life inside her head. A man with thick shadow on his face stood in a doorway and watched her walk by. He was thick set and dressed in a dirty white coat. As she passed, she slipped out of her stilettos and carried on walking, swaying. The man's eyes were cold and he took her in with a glint of pleasure. He moved from the doorway and followed her.

He had an unusual gait, as if he was carrying a gun in his belt, and he had to quicken his pace to gain on Steele. As she turned into a dark side street he grabbed her from behind, clamping his hand over her mouth and dragging her into an alley. He put his other hand inside her blouse and fondled her breasts as she elbowed him in the face. She connected with his nose and he staggered back, his eyes stinging.

Steele kicked him in the groin and was surprised when he moved towards her unhurt. He was reaching in his coat and she kicked at him again, but this time he grabbed her foot and pushed her against the wall. He put his hand up her skirt and pulled out a blackjack.

'Ever been fucked by one of these?', he said.

'I'm a police officer.'

'Even better.'

Steele head butted him, breaking his nose, and as he put his hands to his face she ran from him, out of the alley and down the street.

18

When his father found out, he thrashed him for an hour.

Jackson's legs were so sore he had to swathe the backs of them in gauze for a month before he could sit without wincing. He didn't wash for longer. And when his father asked why he smelt, he thrashed him again. Jackson had beaten up a pupil at the new school so badly the boy was left with a permanent twitch and suspected brain damage.

The new school, the old man's ticket to middle class respectability. Yet all the neighbours hated and feared him, this bruiser with an obvious spell in prison behind him, who couldn't hold his knife and fork correctly. This misfit with the son who turned on their children and frightened them.

He used to go to every school event with a persistence that was both embarrassing and puzzling to Jackson, given his disinterest in most matters that concerned his family. As a child Jackson felt sick of trying to fit into a lifestyle he knew he didn't belong to and he hated his father, resenting his voice and everything about him.

His father, the man who routinely stuck sawn-off

shotguns into bank cashiers' faces. The man who never touched his wife except with the back of his hand.

As Flare reminisced he wondered whether any marriage could survive life with a detective dealing with the darker side of the human psyche on a daily basis. He concluded he was right never to have contemplated it.

He caught his reflection in the mirror, a jaded face in grey, unrecognisable and alien as some ancient sin. He looked at the eyes, the burnt out sockets, the lines crawling upwards like a statement of his guilt and complicity in the acts which he was paid to seek out and end, and he saw the fleeting shadow of his own attraction to mankind's horrors.

He remembered finding the body of a dead dog at the end of the garden as a boy. His father had come upon him there, arms full of compost. He hadn't known how long his father had stood watching him prod the body, staring at the red gash on the dead animal's side, but he recalled his words as clearly as if he'd heard them yesterday.

'That's a grim fascination for a boy, Jackson, and one I suggest you nip in the bud before it takes you over.'

He poured a malt and sat feeling its warmth flood over him in a numbing tide that put the murderers he sought at arm's distance. He felt the line between him and them blur, the sense that they lived next door and were as watchful of him as he was of them, and he struggled with the whisky's slow dissolution of his awareness, as if he wished to return to the full glare of the harsh daylight he lived in, even at night.

He wondered if sleep would come to him. A noise in the street that sounded like a camera shutter forced him to drink deeper from the bottle of Glenlivet. It only brought more memories.

Flare's father had a hobby.

He bought his first Pentax when Jackson was two and proceeded to a Nikon a few years later. He loved it for its professional reputation.

'It's the best camera in the world', he said to Jackson, aged nine. 'Look at it.'

He tossed it at him and Jackson caught it, wondering if the trap was for him to let it fall and be beaten. One entire summer holiday he had to sit on his right buttock because his left was covered in welts caused by his father's belt.

His father left him alone with the camera as he went to fetch a beer, and Jackson peered into the chest he had in the studio that stood at the back of the house. The first drawers contained landscape shots, family portraits, but as he waited for his father to return he looked into the bottom drawer. What he saw brought bile into his mouth.

Shot after shot of semi-nude and nude boys posing awkwardly with fear in their eyes, their bodies frozen with disbelief.

When his father returned Jackson said nothing and left on the excuse of doing some school work. He never mentioned his discovery to anyone, never disclosed the truth about his father to another living being. He watched his mother cower in fear of her husband and he heard her sobbing alone at night.

Samuel Flare was shot dead by police officers when he carried out a bank job after running up so much debt on his obsession with cameras that Jackson and his mother were hungry most of the time.

After the funeral Flare stole into the studio at night and set light to it with a jerry can of petrol. From that day on to him every policeman he passed in the street was a figure of redemption against a dark secret he couldn't forget. He used to search their uniforms in vain for guns. It seemed to him every cop should carry one.

OBJECTS OF DESIRE

19

Jackson, do you think you'll catch me that way?
I belong to a world that excludes you and always has.

Steele was sitting in the all night café she frequented when she wanted to be on her own and avoid the hollowness of her empty flat. After the attack she'd found a pub and stopped her hands trembling with a few brandies. She walked the streets trying to calm the hunger. She had a clear picture of her attacker in her mind. She could see his dead eyes buried in his hard face. She wanted to hurt a man like that. She wanted to make him feel what it was like.

She was finishing her second latte when she heard a familiar voice.

'Hello Mandy.'

It resonated in the air with a frisson of distant memory that made her shudder as she turned slowly to see his clear cut face staring down at her, the same smile, the same charm that lured her into bed all those years ago. She looked around, realising she didn't want to be seen with him.

'Mark.'

The weakness of her voice irritated her.

He sat down.

'How's things?'

'Oh, you know.'

'No, I don't know, Mandy. Remember?'

'Busy.'

'Too busy to call?'

'I'm an Inspector now.'

He looked down at her feet.

'An Inspector with no shoes. Well, Inspector, you never explained why you disappeared like that. I thought we had a good thing going.'

'I moved and lost a lot of contacts.'

'Don't give me that. Show me more respect.'

She looked at him and wavered in her resolution not to let him in. His eyes still held that sparkle and he dressed as sharply as ever, with that intrinsic sense of style she craved. He wasn't part of her world and she wanted him. He could be an object of her desire.

'I'm sorry', she said.

'For what?'

'Leaving like that. I'm not good at commitment.'

'So, are we going to try again?'

20

Designer silk encircles Sandra's pampered skin.
She likes to feel it slide down her waxed legs as she
undresses in erotic twilight.
She walks about her room touching herself, aroused in
Mirrorland.
Martha craves the dark, hiding from the world.
They both enjoy the watchful eyes of strangers,
They need to be seen to feel they exist.

It still lived in her.

Steele had wanted to be a cop for as long as she could remember. When she finally got her badge she realised she was moving in a man's world. And it had its rules. She tried to fit in. Sleeping with her superior officer was never part of the plan. He tried and tried and when she worked late he'd brush against her. She remembered the time she was leaning over the filing cabinet. She felt his hardness pause against her buttocks. He smoked More menthols and after what he did their smell always evoked nausea in her.

She cut her hair until it was so short she thought she

looked like a boy. But she didn't. She still saw the flicker of desire in men's eyes.

When the assault happened, it was dirty and small and mean and trivial. She just wanted to forget about it. It was the stain on the small black dress she'd worn that night he waited for her that stuck in her mind like a fish hook. Several trips to the dry cleaner eliminated it, but not from her memory, and as she tried to remove that, she felt a part of herself ripping, as if the hook was lodged in a vein. But it tainted her faith in the police. She wanted to be part of the force she believed existed when she first decided to become a cop.

She'd been avoiding him all evening. Inspector Allen. He treated all women PC's as hired help and made loud sexist remarks every time one walked into the room. She never thought he'd try what he did.

He came in and grabbed her as she was typing up a report. She said nothing, but as she pulled away he squeezed her breast. He placed his hand between her legs and said 'go on, you want it, that's why you joined.'

She went out into the corridor and waited until he left. Then she got dressed to go out with some of the other women officers. She'd been planning the outing for weeks, tired of the pressure he'd placed her under. She overdid the makeup, and the dress was shorter than those she usually wore. She was making a point to herself.

He was waiting for her in the car park. She had the door of her Mini open and he grabbed her and took out his penis and held it against her leg. She looked down at it and wanted to say something humiliating, but just stood there shaking. Then he pushed her in. She could taste tobacco on his hand as he clamped it to her mouth and raped her. She watched a fly crawl across the roof as he spent himself in her. Afterwards he looked into her eyes for a long time, as if he was measuring how much he'd taken away. She waited until he left. Then she went to the ladies and threw up.

She gave up cigarettes the next day, threw her last pack of Silk Cuts in the bin and never looked back. She gave up a lot that day and let the hunger grow in her until it found its outlet.

As Anne Lacey got into her Mercedes, she felt a hand over her face and passed out. Outside the window a curtain of rain fell.

When she awoke she was staring up at a tall man wearing a balaclava. She was cold and felt concrete on her bare legs.

'I'm not going to hurt you, just scare you a little, OK?'

'Let me go!'

She struggled to her feet, but he pushed her down again.

Dizziness rocked her brain.

'A friend of ours feels he's done enough for you, now you know how bruising hurts, so be a good girl and cooperate.'

'What do you want?'

'Leave him alone.'

'Razor?'

'I didn't say that but you're a clever girl. Money's money, after all.'

'You can't do this.'

'And here's me thinking you were smart.'

He hit her, a sharp slap across the face with the back of his hand, then held her down and pulled up her sleeve. When he left, her arm was heavily bruised.

Her legs were shaking as she got up and walked to her car that was parked at the end of the vacant parking lot.

21

Martha likes petals
Scattered on her bed.
She lies there, a bud of swollen promise ripe for my
plucking.
She hides her soft and hollow lies beneath
The fallen lines that stain her face
With the shallow tide of creeping age, as younger women
take her place.

Steele was ashamed of her flat and the clear sense it gave of the loveless routine of her days.

She let him in, poured them both a vodka and sat on the sofa next to him staring ahead of her.

'Mandy', he said, reaching across and touching her.

She thought of Flare and the abhorrent closeness of him in the car and felt the slow caress of an old hand on the cold skin of her leg. She looked him in the eyes, seeing nothing there of her day to day life. A knot unravelled in her, like the unfurling of a crumpled flag.

'OK Mark', she said, knowing it was a lie, and feeling something pulse within her that she thought was dead, hating her desire.

She turned to look at him. Her police cuffs dangled from the back of a broken chair. She remembered smashing it one day when she felt so frustrated working with Flare she almost took Vic Jones up on his offer. And then it occurred to her that the reason she stayed with Flare was because she was not attracted to him. Vic was another story. She had to desexualize herself to be a cop.

Looking at Mark and knowing what appealed to her she thought of how she had allayed Allen's violation of her belief. For it was as much this as her body she sought to gain control of.

At first it was pleasure she sought, the moment's negation of her isolation, her exile from herself. The years of nameless men. A parade of bodies with no intimacy. She was losing herself further during that time. Until one night she discovered what she wanted.

She could feel Marks's eyes on her as she undressed. She stood up and took off her blouse, looking down at him as she unhooked her bra. It dangled cheaply from the back of the broken chair and she thought of all the wealth women like Martha Fornalski spent on lingerie. She caught her reflection in the mirror over the bed, she looked at her firm breasts, and she could feel his desire. He stood and removed his shirt and trousers and she pulled down her skirt and then her panties, watching this pantomime in reflection.

As Steele lay naked beside Mark his touch soothed some part of her she'd forgotten existed. But then it happened. The reason she'd left.

She looked at him and the old memories returned. She knew she had no option now, knowing the reason she'd invited him back.

As he entered her she felt it and turned him over on his back. It had to be her hands on him.

What she did then made that old memory of herself seem lame, like someone dabbling in it.

And this was real.

When he fought back she surprised herself. He hit her a few times, gentle slaps within the parameters of the game, and she grabbed the cuffs, lashed his wrists to the bed and punched him, squeezing him inside her, pushing down on him with her haunches tight against his skin. She saw the blood she needed beading from his sweat-drenched skin and she felt hot and let it all go and fell back and remembered being flooded with Allen's come in her Mini.

She wanted to hurt him more, and as she looked down at him sexual rage twitched inside her like a raw nerve. She'd opened his skin and she leant and licked the blood from his breast with a gesture that surprised her in its gentleness as she turned and caught her reflection in the mirror by the bed, her face high on what her body needed. She extracted her satisfaction with all the accumulated years of vengeance, pumping with her hips in a wave of self-knowing as she feasted on the pleasure that she brought herself. She injured the memory of it. She drained him and felt herself gushing. She'd made him useless and filled him with her knowledge of the soul's violation and its dark attendant births. She looked at him in satisfaction, and saw his face melt, its left side burnt like raw genitals and she pulled away, scrambling from the bed, watching the image fade, seeing Mark's face again and touching him with cold fingers. As she uncuffed him she wondered why Flare had entered the scarred map of her psyche.

She left him there and ran a bath. But Flare's image wouldn't leave her. Memories invaded her mind.

Sometimes she would sit watching him when, legs on his desk and on the phone, he had his back turned. It was a rare event, as if he didn't like being observed, and she would eye him with a close scrutiny born of her latent discomfort with this man she called her partner.

It wasn't the mark, not his face, but his anger that unnerved her the most. He made her flesh crawl and sometimes she felt he was weighing up her desirability, imagining what she was like in bed. When this thought rose from her psyche she had to suppress a shudder, as if she was witnessing some sick design of her own, an agenda bent on her own destruction, a wilful anchoring of her thoughts to her hatred for men.

He hated her. That was it, he hated her and wanted to harm her.

An acrid smell rose like a polluted tide into her nostrils, summoning a flood of bile.

That evening Martha Fornalski returned late from a dinner with Sandra Gould.

She stood in the glare of the sensor lights, inserted

her key in the front door, and walked into the huge hallway, where she pondered the emptiness of her home before going upstairs to undress.

As she hung up her clothes she felt a draught of cold air on her skin. She wrapped her arms around her body, catching her own reflection in the mirror. She wondered if the colour of her bra and panties suited her and she thought about shopping. Then she saw a black shadow move behind her.

She barely saw the visible part of his face before he clamped his gloved hand over her mouth and she found herself staring at the ceiling. He looked down at her and she thought how beautiful the mask he wore was.

His voice invaded her like a murderous mantra.

'Martha I know your body, you have shown it to me many times', he said. 'I know the shape of your breasts and how you like to masturbate, you little show thing, my piece of porn, your loving days are done.'

He said it almost as if he was singing a song, but there were no notes in his voice, and she struggled to identify what it was that was so familiar in the cold metal whisper that emanated from his mouth. She felt something sharp tear her and a warmth spreading across her body. She struggled, kicking out.

The figure in the room leant down and inserted something deep inside her, flooding the carpet with her blood. She watched it bubble on the tiny filaments of hair.

She felt him cut her neck. He moved away and she

searched the night for his face, drifting. She could hear the noise of glass shattering in the bathroom.

'Do you like my Swarovski mask?', he said. 'It would grace a masquerade ball, the design is flawless and complements the crystals.'

Martha's killer proceeded to cut a part of her away which he took with him, leaving her lying like some used shell whose husk contained the vital thing he sought.

THE DISCRETION OF LINGERIE

22

Michael McKleith stood at six foot four. He had a boxer's build and the trademark nose.

The prison guard looked dwarfed next to him, as he ushered him into the office. From time to time he glanced at McKleith, whose face was as hard as rock.

'Sign', he said, passing him a pen, watching as McKleith bent over the papers and scrawled his name.

The guard handed him the things he came in with, objects from another lifetime passed over a broken counter called freedom. McKleith eyed the hinge, which hung uselessly beneath the chipped plywood, and inspected his property with indifference, counted his money, and placed the items in the pocket of his faded denim jacket. Only his Zippo lighter seemed of interest to him, and he turned it over in his palm.

'I don't need to tell you I hope we don't see you again', the guard said.

'You won't.'

He led him out into the bright sunshine.

McKleith stood at the gates of Wandsworth prison as they were shut behind him, looking around the deserted street and up at the sky in which distant birds wheeled. A woman passed by, eyeing him disapprovingly and McKleith stared her down. Then he walked to Tooting Bec station where he bought a packet of Marlboros.

He stood on the platform looking for his destination. As the train approached he flicked open his Zippo and smiled as it ignited. He lit a cigarette and got on, sitting with it alight in his mouth.

The carriage was empty, apart from a man who sat on the chair opposite. He glanced at the no smoking sign.

'You got a problem?', McKleith said.

'Yes, yes, I do as it happens', the man said, folding his copy of The Independent. 'It says no smoking.'

He pointed at the sign.

McKleith narrowed his eyes and took a long drag, then removed his cigarette from his mouth and held it in the air between them.

'And you think I'm going to put it out because of that?'

'That would be the decent thing to do.'

'Decent?'

'It's also the law.'

'Law. Interesting word law.'

'Look, are you going to put it out or not? I can always call the security guard.'

'You see, the law as it stands is nothing more than a collection of moralising shit dreamt up by idiots like you. People at the top break it all the time, people at the bottom do that and they're punished.'

'I'm not going to sit here and listen to you spout off

about what you think of the law. We live in a society where there are laws whether you like it or not. Now are you going to put that out?'

McKleith put the cigarette back in his mouth and dragged on it, keeping the man fixed firmly in his stare.

'Right, I'm calling the guard. There's one in the next carriage.'

McKleith stood up.

'I've had enough of guards and I've had enough of you.'

He stood in front of him, blocking his passage.

'Get out of my way.'

'Sit down.'

The man tried to push past him but McKleith grabbed him by the collar and forced him back into his seat.

'What do you think you're doing?'

'Sit there and shut up or I'll hurt you, and believe me I'm good at hurting people.'

'Are you threatening me?'

'Yes, I am threatening you.'

McKleith slapped him across the cheek. It was a hard slap which produced shock and outrage in the man's face. Then he pushed him further back into his seat, his clenched fist deep in his chest as he gripped and twisted his suit, pressing his knuckles into him.

'Got it?'

The man nodded.

McKleith pulled out his lighter.

'See this? It's a Zippo, classic. See the flame? Feel it? It burns doesn't it? Stop wriggling.'

He singed the man's cheek.

'Now shut up.'

McKleith sat down and finished his cigarette and watched as the man got off at the next station. Then he swung his legs up on the vacant seat and read the ads that lined the wall.

When the Embankment swung into view he got off and changed trains for Earl's Court.

At nine o'clock Sandra Gould went downstairs. She checked her messages and then got her Fendi Selleria sable handbag.

As she opened the front door she felt it pushed forcibly from the outside. She was knocked back and fell onto the hallway tiles.

She heard the door slam shut and looked up at the masked figure standing over her.

'It's you', she said.

Then she started to scream. He reached down and took hold of her neck, choking the sound, as her nails clawed uselessly at the black leather.

'Sandra, you've snagged one, let me help', he said, tearing the broken nail from her finger.

With his other hand he lifted her Versace skirt. He paused to take in her flesh and then tore open her blouse. He reached a hand inside the cup of her Myla

Cherie bra, squeezing her left breast. He looked into her face.

'So you see through the mask, I am sure you like hiding. You like being watched?'

She shook her head, her eyes staring wildly at him, like a tethered mare witnessing the murder of her foal.

'Nice tits, large round nipples you have', he said, running his finger around them. 'They're getting hard, are you getting wet? What does make you wet? Showing yourself to men?'

She kicked out and he pinned her to the floor. Then he pulled something from his pocket that flashed in the lights and he began to cut her. She turned from him, noticing the pool of blood at her side. He pulled a mirror from his pocket and forced Sandra's head towards it, so she was staring at her own mutilation.

'Welcome to Mirrorland, where all your fantasies are fulfilled. You have made a brand of your image and now I am going to redesign you.'

He cut her Versace skirt from her and carved something into her neck. Then he inserted the weapon deep into her chest. She gazed at him, wondering what was real in the land of Glamour. One hand held her neck and her head was pinioned to the floor. Then he put his other hand into the wound and dug deep inside her.

She thought of her old gynaecologist Dr. Morris, a mild man whose placid face would change as he examined her.

'Watch me', he said. 'Ah, don't look away, watchfulness is all you have at the end of the day.'

She was drifting as he removed his hand from her mouth. She saw her face in the mirror, a mute witness to this grim act. And her killer dragged from her some dripping thing that once sustained her, which he placed to one side before returning the knife to her and severing her carotid artery, standing and watching as she pumped away the last life left within her. He tightened her Hermes scarf deep into the wound and took a length of rope from his bag, which he attached to the scarf. He hoisted it through the banisters on the first landing of the violated mansion and lifted Sandra so she was standing.

He placed what he'd removed from her in a clear plastic bag. Then he moved to the door carrying what he came there for, leaving the way he came.

23

The night Harlan White attacked Steele he'd been on his way to Acton. He'd met a business associate for some supper and was walking to his Mercedes when he stopped to have a cigarette and stood in the doorway of a shop to watch for women. For women were his trade. He still pimped and was a casual rapist.

Flare's mutilation of him had turned him into an object rapist. He favoured blunt objects, his blackjack being the weapon he used the most, since it was portable, but he had an array of police truncheons he loved using, as well as rolling pins and pieces of wood that left splinters in his victims. It was not beneath him to use sharp objects, and he'd also used broken bottles, knives, drill bits and shards of glass, but the mess was a problem. He didn't want to stain his clothes, especially the dirty white coat he wore like a uniform.

Harlan White often thought about getting Flare killed. He knew hit men and had the money. But he fancied doing something worse, and he needed to accrue enough money for that. He wanted to kidnap Flare. He wanted to lock him up and torture him. So he decided to set up a new brothel.

The business associate he'd met was connected to

Eastern European gangs who were bringing in illegal immigrants, all women, and sending them to houses from which they never escaped. The women were young, believed they were going to the UK to get work, and were locked in rooms where they were given drugs or beaten to ensure compliance with the series of punters who queued up to have sex with them.

White saw this as a way to make the kind of money he needed to exact vengeance on Flare. He could rape them as well, satisfying the addiction Flare had given him. Steele was one of many women he'd assaulted in empty nocturnal streets and he was annoyed she had got away.

That night he'd spent four hours in A&E waiting to get his nose fixed. He also had a blood stain on his white coat which created an inner rage in him.

But the deal had been struck with his contact and the next day a lorryful of women turned up at the house he'd bought in Acton. They were taken in under cover of night. He and his associate took them to their rooms which they promptly locked. That night White raped one of them with the heel of her stiletto shoe.

24

Alan Palmer was the leading journalist if you wanted to expose a celebrity. He'd cut his teeth on The Sun and now freelanced for all the leading newspapers and magazines. That morning Anne Lacey met him at his office in Fleet Street. She handed him the pictures of her injuries and gave him the full story. He leaned back in his swivel chair, keeping his eyes fixed firmly on her face, making sure he didn't lower his gaze.

'This is a big one', he said.

'I know.'

'So Razor did that to you?'

'Yup. And hired someone to do this.'

She rolled up her sleeve. He leaned forward and looked at the fresh bruises.

'Can you prove that?'

'That he hired someone? No.'

'I'll run the first story then, see what comes back.'

'He's got a serious coke problem.'

'I'll put it in.'

He handed her an envelope which she opened and counted the cash.

As she stood up to go he said 'Did you know he's got previous?'

'No.'

'Assaulted a girlfriend a few years ago.'

'Doesn't surprise me.'

She left and drove to her shoot as Alan Palmer scanned the pictures into his computer and prepared the story.

Returning from the shops Gertrude Miller inspected herself in the hallway mirror.

She scraped her hair back until her skin was pulled so tight across her forehead it raised her eyebrows. She turned her face to one side and then the other. She looked deep into her own eyes. She straightened her starched dress and pulled the collar of her blouse a little tighter around her neck. Then she looked at the broach that was pinned to her jacket and removed it.

The clock told her it was time to prepare dinner and she walked into the kitchen. Occasionally she looked out of the window, alerted by a noise. On seeing it was an animal or the wind she'd relax and continue with what she was doing. She cut the rabbit into strips and began the marination, dipping her hands deep into the rich mixture.

She massaged and kneaded the cold flesh until it was warm beneath her fingertips, enjoying the squelch of the succulent sauce. She pressed against the work surface, getting closer to the food. When she finished, she ran her hands under the tap for a long time, watching the blood thin and fade in the sink.

Then she placed the lid on the pan, cleaned the kitchen, and went upstairs. She stood beneath the bathroom light inspecting her hands, turning them over and over, as if searching for a clue.

25

Martha Fornalski's housekeeper found her body. Cleaning her way through the house, she entered the darkened bedroom, vacuum cleaner in hand, and slipped in Martha's blood. Her screams could be heard in the neighbouring gardens, where startled householders dropped hoses and gardening shears and stared into the air.

The morning Flare and Steele went to the murder scene London was grey. A blanket of cloud hung overhead with no sun.

'If he's gone back to kill Fornalski's wife it backs up one theory', Flare said as he drove there.

'What, that the killer knows these people?'

'That he knows them well, that he's done business with them.'

Steele thought for a moment.

'OK, say he's mixed with this crowd and for whatever reasons he's killed two of them, why kill Martha?'

'She might guess he's behind it.'

'He's silencing her.'

'Yes.'

'Or maybe she knows whatever it is he doesn't want to get out.'

'That's a strong possibility.'

He pulled onto the drive and they passed through the police cordons and donned protective clothing. Maurice Ray was already there and Flare and Steele walked upstairs and entered the bedroom as the flashlight of Ray's police issue Nikon D300 camera blasted light at the body on the floor.

'The scene's contaminated', Ray said. 'The maid made a mess on the spatter.'

The dried blood had made a dark map of the killer's mood on the carpet where Martha Fornalski lay open like an abandoned autopsy. Her mouth was blackened. Flare looked down at the killer's handiwork. The wound in her throat was as deep as a river bed.

'He's not just content with killing them, is he?', Steele said.

'I think we've just stepped off the precipice into his pathology.'

'What's that he's cut into her neck?'

Flare looked at the letter.

'It's an H this time.'

'Another brand?'

As they inspected the room Steele saw the shattered glass on the bathroom tiles.

'Something's been smashed in here', she said. 'It looks like a perfume bottle.'

'Hermes', Flare said. 'This guy's hung up on designer goods.'

They made a tour of the house, finding no sign of a break in.

'He was inside when she got home', Flare said.

'So we interview everyone in the Fornalskis' immediate circle.'

'Everyone who has keys to the house.'

They spoke to the housekeeper, who said that the gardener had keys to the outside only and she was the main key bearer. Then they went back to the station to begin compiling the list of suspects.

I know their little ways and the catchphrase they use,
Their ticket to their exclusive club.

26

Sandra Gould's body wasn't discovered until the next day when the postman tried to jam a parcel through her letterbox. He noticed a trail of blood leading across the hallway and called the police on his mobile.

Flare and Steele had to walk around the edge of the tiled hallway not to tread in the spatter.

It was clear what the killer had removed. Sandra's chest lay open as if someone had stretched it like a piece of meat. Her aorta jutted out of her Versace blouse like a severed pipe.

Maurice Ray was gathering information and to Steele he looked sinister behind his mask. It seemed to hide something about him and she thought how easy it was for him to witness scenes of extreme violence. His detachment from the suffering made him questionable. She wondered if he had any sexual desire for women.

'He must have broken her ribs to do that', Flare said.

'How much physical strength does it take to remove a heart?', Steele said.

'He removes her skirt and pulls down her bra, then he cuts her open and hangs her.'

'By her designer scarf.'

Maurice Ray stood up and walked over to them, his shoe covers rustling on the floor.

'A lot, to answer your question', he said to Steele. 'This killer is extremely strong to have torn her chest open like that.'

Steele looked into his eyes and wondered what shade of green they were. They seemed unlike any colour she had ever seen and she thought it strange she hadn't noticed them before. It occurred to her that Maurice Ray wore contact lenses and his eyes changed colour. His sexuality was an irritation to her and she wanted to penetrate it.

It was raining hard as they made a tour of the garden, looking for the killer's entry point.

'This weather's going to wash any evidence away', Flare said.

Back at the station he called Don Harvard.

'He'll be in this afternoon', he said, putting down the phone.

'Why do you think he went back for the wives?', Steele said.

'They know something about him.'

'Then why not kill them right off?'

'Maybe he couldn't get access to them.'

'Or something happened after he killed their husbands.'

'Like what?'

'They knew he was the killer and they blackmailed him.'

'Which makes both Martha Fornalski and Sandra

Gould somehow complicit in the murders of their husbands.'

'It also indicates money as a motive.'

'The wives after their husbands' money?'

'Maybe they wanted them dead, were in it with the killer and then they did something to piss him off.'

'A hit man? They don't kill like this', Flare said.

'Unless he wants to throw us off the track, in which case we've got a game player.'

'These killers are all game players.'

Michael McKleith found a room in a boarding house at the edge of Earl's Court, between the Aussie pubs and the rows of neglected Victorian houses that lined Baron's Court.

From the grimy privacy of his quarters he began to plan his future. He tracked down a couple of old contacts, guys who were good at finding people. He waited.

Every day he bought a copy of The Sun. Inside one was a story about Razor. The headline was very simple.

'Razor the basher', it said.

It contained a picture of him staggering out of a pub. The article went into more detail.

'Razor the rabid rock star has a habit of beating up his girlfriends, a side of his personality he keeps well out of the limelight. Anne Lacey, the model, bears the bruises from his latest episode, and he's done it before. High on coke, he lashes out and inflicts the injuries shown here. What a role model.'

When he read it, Razor threw his TV across the room. Then he rang his press agent and his lawyer.

Frank Norris looked indifferently at Steele as she said 'He's almost hacked her head off.'

He was examining the body of Martha Fornalski and as he did Steele took in her figure, blighted now by the killer's mutilations.

'He slashed her throat and removed her tongue', Norris said. 'He cut it back to the Palatine Tonsil, pretty neat work too.'

'Do you know what weapon he used?', Flare said.

'I'd say he used a surgical clamp and a scalpel. He carved the letter into her neck far enough away from the wound. I have the other victim here, also with a letter on her neck.'

He moved over to another table and showed them Sandra Gould.

Steele stared at her waxed vagina, her lower half a piece of pure sexual appeal shadowed by her mutilated torso.

'He cut her carotid artery and removed her heart', Norris said. 'He was fairly brutal with the excision this time in the way he severed her aorta.'

That afternoon Don Harvard turned up at the station. He could see the weariness written on Flare's face.

'The fact that the killer is removing parts of their anatomy indicates this is not about money', he said, setting his papers down.

'Or it's something he's doing to throw us off his scent', Flare said. 'He's gone after the wives because they know him.'

Harvard shook his head.

'Make it look like some pathology he doesn't have?', he said.

'Yes. Why kill Martha Fornalski and Sandra Gould, why take the risk? Say it is about money and they've guessed who killed their husbands, something's gone on between them and the killer, he wants them out of the way.'

'You mean they were blackmailing him?'

'Could be.'

'I don't think so.'

'Well, if he wants to kill the wives, why not just do both couples at the same time?', Steele said.

'His mind doesn't work like that.'

'I think this is about a set, a lifestyle we aren't part of, and which has its own rules. I think behind these murders is a business deal gone wrong', Flare said.

'I don't.'

'He's part of their set', Flare said.

'No.'

'OK Don, so what do you think?'

'The way he's butchering these victims, the way he's removing their body parts belongs to a very particular form of pathology.'

'What if it's part of his line of work?' Steele said.

'You mean he's a surgeon?'

'Maybe.'

'Unlikely.'

'So go on Don', Flare said.

'There are layers to this man's psyche that are only beginning to open up and they're doing so through the killings. What we do have is his obsession with the victims' bodies.'

'I've seen my share of murder victims', Flare said, 'and it's all about control at the end of the day, controlling to the point of death.'

'Of course, but this is different. He's a collector.'

'Of what?', Steele said.

'Body parts.'

'You mean he's keeping them?'

'Not in the way you think. He's using them.'

'Using how?', Flare said.

'That we don't know yet. But I've studied the wounding and the way he's cutting them. There's a hunger, there's a need. He's taking parts of them away for a purpose, and therein lies the key to finding him.'

'What uses are there?'

'I'm not talking black market sales here, I'm talking the need for these parts in his psyche.'

'And the letters he's cutting into them.'

'Designer brands and branding. He cut the letter H of Hermes into Martha Fornalski's neck, the location of the letters is significant. He smashed a bottle of Hermes perfume, there is a picture emerging.'

'He also hanged Sandra Gould with a Hermes scarf.'

'Hermes was the messenger, but I don't think is about mythology, I think it's about habits. The habits of his victims. He cut the letter V into Sandra Gould's neck, it's the V of Versace. Frank says Martha was wearing Damaris lingerie.'

'Was Sandra Gould wearing Bordelle?'

'No. But I suggest you find out whether she has any in her wardrobe.'

'What does this say?', Steele said.

'The killer is making a point of saying he knows what his male victims' wives like to wear, that he has knowledge of their erotic lives.'

BLEACH AND RAZOR BLADES

27

The Herefords sat at their table at The Ivy. They'd been going there for years and knew the waiters by their first names. Max turned over the menu lazily, gazing at Lucinda, who was choosing her hors d'oeuvre. She looked like a picture set in cream, immaculate, her figure complimented by her Valentino dress. Her rich brown hair shone beneath the subdued lights.

He thought what an attractive woman she was.

'May I offer you some bread, Sir?', the waiter said, approaching to his left.

'Thank you Neville.'

He reached for a granary slice and looked across the white tablecloth at Lucinda.

'Darling?'

Neville paused at her elbow, basket of freshly baked bread on offer.

'It smells delicious, but, must watch the figure.'

'Darling, your figure is always perfect', Max said.

As Max ordered drinks, Lucinda noticed Paul and Samantha DeLonge enter.

'Oh darling, shall we ask them to join us?', she said, 'it's been ages.'

She waved and they came over. Samantha was

wearing a cocktail dress that Max thought complimented her cleavage.

'You both look well', he said.

'Lovely to see you', Samantha said, as she air-kissed him.

Lucinda showed Paul her cheek.

'Now where did you get those tans?', she said.

'A couple of weeks in the Bahamas.'

'How fantastic, join us?'

'Love to.'

Lucinda looked at Samantha, whose blonde hair caressed her brown shoulders, and she wondered if Max found her more attractive.

As they enjoyed a leisurely dinner, feasting on game and various cuts of offal, Gertrude Miller put the finishing touches to a steak and kidney pie she'd made for Ben, who was returning from his business trip. She'd lovingly selected the finest cuts of meat and made the sauce thick and strong, with a plentiful supply of kidney, which Ben was particularly partial to. She opened the kitchen cupboard and inspected the contents of a box of kitchen knives she'd bought from Sainsbury's. Then she took them outside and placed them in the boot of her car.

At six o'clock she went upstairs to see how Maxwell and Mary were progressing with their homework. Both sat with heads bowed and she left their rooms satisfied. She changed into a low cut dress and went downstairs to wait for Ben's return.

She turned on the news. The police crackdown on

prostitution was being covered. The announcer said: 'Women are being held and routinely questioned about their involvement with these gangs. Many of them are victims who have broken the law through drug deals that are connected to the problems we see on our streets. This is going to be a long operation.'

She aimed the remote control at the set like a gun and switched it off.

She went through to the hall and stood listening for any sound from upstairs. Catching her reflection in the mirror she went up to the bedroom and took her dress off. Then she pulled her grey skirt and starched white blouse out of the cupboard and walked through to the bathroom with these slung over her arm.

She put the light on and stood staring at her naked body in front of the mirror. She lifted and let fall her breasts. She reached into the bathroom cabinet and found a long needle which she used to lance the children's boils. Turning round she gripped one of her buttocks. She pressed the needle deep into it and pulled it out, watching the bead of blood form there.

She placed a plaster over it, got dressed, washed the needle, and went downstairs, where she sat waiting for Ben. When he returned Maxwell and Mary were waiting for him in the living room and he hugged them both. Gertrude came into the hallway and held her cheek out to him.

'Good trip?', she said.

'Very good. And have you two been behaving yourselves?'

'Yes, daddy.'

'Talking in chorus now.'

'I have something special in the oven for you', Gertrude said.

'What is it?'

'Steak and kidney.'

They followed Gertrude through to the kitchen where she served them. She sat and ate a little and when she stood up to clear the table she noticed a small patch of blood had soaked through her skirt and stained the chair. As Ben watched TV with Mary and Maxwell she scoured and scrubbed the patch as if she were trying to remove herself from the family, before going upstairs and sitting in the darkened bedroom.

28

Sandra Gould's wardrobe contained a lot of items from Bordelle. She liked their Bettie bras and waist briefs, and she'd owned some leather cuffs and ring nipplets.

'It's a style of lingerie a woman who enjoys bondage might buy', Harvard said. 'Psychologically it tells us a lot about her. Her husband must have known because she wasn't hiding them.'

'Does it give us any clues about the killer?', Flare said.

'He's obviously interested in what lingerie his female victims wear, which is connected to his sexual obsession about them. Whether that means he's into bondage or opposed to it is another matter.'

Razor's lawyer threatened The Sun with a lawsuit, while Razor got high and thought about killing Anne Lacey.

He found some of her clothes in his wardrobe and threw these out into the street below where some passing tourists ran off with them. He picked up two groupies and took them back to his flat where he had a long sex session, but couldn't shake off his rage with Anne.

Finally, at two o'clock in the morning he drove round

to her flat and sat outside looking up at her window. No lights. He walked to her door and raised his hand to ring her bell when, finger poised mid air, he walked away. As he was about to get into his car he saw a skip overflowing with bricks. He picked one up and hurled it at her window and heard the glass shatter, shards flying out and landing in the street.

He got in his Gallardo and burnt tyre marks straight down the middle of the street.

Michael McKleith sat in the corner of The Bell.

He'd been nursing his pint for an hour when he saw his old drinking partner come in.

'All right Mike?'

'Tom.'

'Another one?'

'Wouldn't mind.'

He handed him his glass.

He watched as Tom pushed two men aside at the bar. They looked round angrily and then turned their backs once they'd got a good look at his hulking form.

Tom was well over six foot, covered in tattoos, and he had a scar that ran down the side of his face. He looked permanently angry.

'I owe you one from the nick', he said, sitting down.

McKleith took a deep sip of bitter.

'Owe me?'

'For taking care of that screw that time.'

'That.'

'You did him good and proper.'

'Yeah, well, he was a fuckin screw wasn't he?'

'Good to see you Mike, how you keeping?'

'Just got out, ain't I?'

'Yeah I heard.'

'An I need a little extra.'

'So you need a piece.'

'Heard you can fix me up with one.'

'Planning something special?'

'Just a small job.'

'One man?'

'For the moment.'

He handed him a plastic bag.

McKleith examined the contents under the table.

'It'll do the job', Tom said.

'How much?'

'Hundred.'

'All right.'

Rain fell heavily that night as Ben found himself falling into a deep sleep.

Gertrude stood over him and held his hand. There was little tenderness in the gesture. She looked like a bedside nurse inspecting a patient's pulse. After a while she let his arm drop.

He didn't stir as she pushed him in the shoulder, rousing only a deep snore. Beside him lay an empty cup which she took downstairs, past the sleeping children, watchful of every creak. Her hands looked like a faint blur as she washed it at the kitchen sink, pouring the residue of white powder at its bottom down the plug hole and rinsing it several times before drying it thoroughly and putting it away.

As the rain fell Flare stayed behind at the station, searching for Harlan White on the internet. He'd been haunted by the fact that he got away ever since the killings began and he thought of what White was capable of inflicting on his victims, as images of the dead women in the basement flashed through his mind.

As this killer who targeted the wealthy eluded them, Flare searched for relief from his frustration and he found it. That night he located an address for White.

29

Flare and Steele were making slow progress with their list of suspects. They'd spoken to the Herefords and the DeLonges, who'd been brief with them. The ranks had closed and they found the circle around the Fornalskis and Goulds uncommunicative.

'They're harbouring a secret', Flare said, leaning across Steele's desk.

'Could be the way these people are.'

'What, unwilling to cooperate with the police?'

'No, private.'

'They're hiding something.'

'Maybe they don't want to let you in.'

'What's that mean?'

She felt his eyes boring into her and she reached hard for her work persona, which had been slipping from her grasp like soap since the other night.

'I've been digging. One of their group, Jack Martins, has a reputation', she said.

'For what?'

'Screwing around.'

'And?'

'I got the distinct sense the other day that one of

the wives was uncomfortable when I mentioned her lunches with Martha Fornalski.'

'Samantha DeLonge.'

'Yes. I asked if there were any other men in Martha's life and she looked away. Which she did again when I mentioned Jack Martins's name.'

'You think there's something there?'

'It's worth finding out.'

'Say she had an affair with him, we know this is no ordinary murder, no crime of passion.'

'I'm not suggesting for a minute Martins had anything to do with the murders, but I think by questioning him, we may find out more about these people and the world they move in.'

'Even if it's a red herring?'

'Even if it's a red herring. Guys like him stick it in anything that spreads its legs, they think they can do what they want with women.'

'And?'

'He'll know their secrets.'

Steele held Flare's stare. She didn't like his proximity to her, he was too close.

He went to his desk and picked up the phone as Steele's personal mobile flashed a message from her open drawer. It was from Mark, and all it said was 'Meet me'. She deleted it and left the office to get a coffee, thinking she needed something stronger to push the memory of the other night away.

That afternoon Flare found a nice skeleton in

Martins's closet. As a young man he'd been arrested on fraud charges.

'He was accused of embezzling money from a company he worked for', he said to Steele.

'What happened?'

'They couldn't prove it. He was never tried.'

'Then we've got something on him.'

'I say we bring him in and use it.'

Their mouths hang open
Like animals' at the abattoir.

DOUBLE LIVES

30

One way for their husbands another for their lovers,
These women seek a special kind of pleasure,
Their branded skins,
Their hidden erotic places,
Their designer clothes arousing them
Beneath lunch tables
And the watchful eye
Of the camera lens.

The address Flare had for White was 26 Barlow Road, Acton. It was his newly acquired house now filled with women who were being raped into prostitutes.

Flare took a drive past it one evening on his way back from the station and sat outside looking at the lights, wanting a sighting of White. He drove round to the Redbrook Tavern and sat in a corner sipping whisky before he returned home. If he had waited he would have seen White walk from his house to Steynes Road, where the tavern was located. He often took this route to buy pizza.

As White turned into Steynes Road that evening he stopped outside a doorway which had caught his attention a few days before as he sat in the Tavern drinking. He'd seen men entering and leaving the address and suspected it was a brothel. He didn't want any rivals on his patch. So that evening he rang the buzzer.

There was no answer.

As he returned to Barlow Road with pizza he saw Gertrude leave her flat. She was getting in her car a few roads away when White laid his hand on the door.

'I want to do business with you', he said.

'Business?'

'You know.'

He looked down at her breasts and Gertrude pulled her coat around her.

'Get your hand off my door.'

White refused to move, so Gertrude started the engine and drove away.

31

Michael McKleith left his shabby room and went down the staircase to the hallway which smelt of old food and dust. He opened the door and walked away from Earl's Court. Once the volume of people on the stained London pavements thinned, he entered a side street and inspected the parked cars. He paused by an old Ford Mondeo on which the road tax had expired. Then he walked towards Bishop's Park, stopping by a small Post Office. Inside an old Indian man served customers behind the cracked glass, while a teenager shunted boxes back and forth.

McKleith noticed the time: 12.30.

There were only two customers in the shop, an old lady and a young man. McKleith bought a copy of The Sun, checked for CCTV cameras and left, walking round the block to see how busy the surrounding streets were. As he disappeared into a crowd, Gertrude Miller left the B&Q store with the wallpaper and carpet. She drove to the flat and proceeded to paste the walls and put up the new look: a simple patternless paper, clinical and clean.

She finished by lunchtime and looked at her handiwork admiringly. She made herself some tea and then moved the bed, leaning it up against the wall. She took the table out into the hall. She laid the carpet and put the furniture back.

Jack Martins was at his golf club when Flare and Steele pulled him in for questioning and he was furious as hell to be shown up like this in front of his friends and associates. He called his lawyer from the back of the car and sat in taciturn silence while he waited for him to arrive. Lucas Stacey was a partner at Bindmans and handled some of the biggest names in London. As soon as he arrived at the station he demanded to know the basis for the arrest.

'We're investigating the murders of Larry and Martha Fornalski and Martin and Sandra Gould', Flare said, eyeing him with cold disdain.

'Which has absolutely nothing to do with my client.'

'Well, then we'll establish that.'

'You don't have anything on him, you don't have any leads on the case and this is the best you can do?'

Stacey held Flare's gaze with his ice blue eyes. Flare turned his attention to Martins.

'How closely did you know Martha Fornalski?'

Martins leaned back and folded his arms.

'She was a friend.'

'How close a friend?'

He glanced at Steele, who thought he exhibited the confidence of a serial philanderer.

'I knew her - well', he said.

She looked at the carefully selected colours he wore, the balance between style and unaggressive masculinity, and for a brief second she wondered what he was like in bed. There was something timeless about him, as if DNA had conspired to give him everything considered handsome in a man. He was tanned and athletic and subtle and dangerous. He had a blonde fire about him and his blue eyes shone with sexual innuendo. Yet there was a tremendous grace in the way he moved, his gestures were polished and seductive. Steele watched as he laid one hand on the table and the other on his lap. She imagined his fingers touching her, and she resented him. He represented something inaccessible and alien to her, like an exotic brand she'd read about in magazines but couldn't afford, and she wanted to press his face into the interview table.

She pictured gripping the back of his neck, her hand holding his in a lock, her hips jammed in the back of his buttocks. His eyes sparkled knowingly and she turned away.

'Did you have an affair with her?', Flare said.

Martins looked at his lawyer.

'What has that got do with anything?', Stacey said.

Flare kept his attention on Martins.

'Cooperate with us and we'll let you go', he said.

Martins paused for a minute.

'Yes, we had an affair, a long time ago.'

'How long?'

'A year.'

'Who ended it?', Steele said.

'It was mutual.'

'No such thing, who ended it?'

'Look, Detective Steele, I don't know how your relationships have gone, but all this is a bit childish. Relationships can come to a close mutually when people are adults.'

'I think she dumped you and you got angry.'

'That's not how it happened.'

'What was it, you weren't up to scratch in bed, she wanted someone younger?'

'I don't need to rise to that particular bait, it's very revealing of you, but you're going to have to do better than that.'

'You're a bit old to be a gigolo, aren't you?'

'Is that how you see me? That says more about you than me.'

'You got angry and killed her.'

'No, I think you're angry Detective Steele, and I can guess why.'

Stacey glanced at him.

'Where were you on the night she was murdered?', Flare said.

'Do I really have to answer this?'

'Yes.'

'You know I'm not the killer, is this really how you police Britain?'

'Answer the question, Mr. Martins.'

'Very well. I was with a woman.'

'Who?'

'She's married.'

'Give us her name and if we can verify your alibi then we'll let you go.'

'Lucinda Hereford. We were at my Mayfair flat.'

'I need her address and number.'

Flare handed him a pad.

It checked out.

It seemed Martins hopped from affair to affair and was with Lucinda on the night Sandra Gould was murdered.

When they questioned her she said 'we were together from six till the small hours.'

'We better release Martins', Flare said to Steele, 'before Lucas Stacey cuts us up into small pieces.'

'You think we'll get anything out of this?'

'Well, we've slapped the water. Let's see which fish jump out.'

32

White was making money fast. Several thousand a day. Soon he'd have enough to kidnap Flare. He spent his evenings raping the women who weren't busy.

The prostitute round the corner still annoyed him and he decided to pay her another visit. As he left and walked to Steyne Road he looked like a stained white blur to Flare who sat in his car watching him.

Steele had stayed behind to catch up on some paperwork. As she was leaving the station she felt a hand on her shoulder.

'Fancy a drink?', Vic Jones said.

She was about to say no when she noticed another message from Mark on her mobile.

'Call me' it read, and she deleted it.

'OK', she said.

'There's this new wine bar up the road, fancy it?'

'Doesn't sound your style Vic.'

'I know my Chardonnay Mandy.'

They found a table in a corner and Steele knocked her first glass back.

'In a hurry?', Vic said.

'You worried I can out drink you?'

They were four bottles down when she felt his hand on her leg and looked at his face, relieved at his looks. He was a handsome man with a touch of viciousness she liked and she began to wonder what he looked like handcuffed naked to a bed.

'What do you think I'll do if you move that further up my leg Vic?'

He inched upwards and felt her hand on his crutch.

'I can feel what you've got, want to show it to me Inspector?'

At her flat she listened to two messages from Mark while Vic was in the toilet, then deleted them.

As they drank Smirnoff Vic tried to kiss her. Steele put her hand on his chest.

'No mouths except down there', she said.

Steele began to strip him hurriedly, getting down to his briefs before he'd even undone her bra. As he touched her breasts she grabbed his cock and began masturbating him vigorously.

Vic pulled down her panties and stuck a finger inside her. She pulled him onto the bed.

'Do you mind?', she said, holding up her cuffs.

He started laughing.

'You're a real cop, what is this, bondage?'

'Just let me cuff you and then I'm going to fuck you, you never done it before?'

'No Mandy.'

She shackled him to the bed, and touched him again.

'Why does every woman these days shave her snatch?', he said.

'It's cleaner, you get to see it all, look.'

She raised a leg and masturbated as she straddled him.

'Now give me it.'

As she sat down on his cock she punched him, drawing a gasp from him.

She was surprised at how aroused she was and began pumping up and down on her haunches, touching her nipples. As Vic pushed upwards she punched him again, catching his nose with the edge of her ring and bending to lick the blood from him. His legs were wet as she slid off him and poured a glass of vodka, watching him there on the bed.

'I suppose you want me to finish you off', she said.

'Let me up Mandy.'

She sat drinking, watching him. Then she walked over with the key which she dangled in front of him.

'Why?'

'Because I didn't agree to this.'

'No you didn't.'

'Undo them.'

She reached down and removed the cuffs and turned her back. Vic dressed and walked over to her.

'You're a sick fucking bitch.'

He slapped her hard across the face. Mandy smashed the bottle against the side of his head and hit him. Vic punched her, knocking her to the floor and left. She got to her feet and went to close the door, seeing a trail of blood across the hallway.

White was drinking in The Redbrook Tavern as he watched Gertrude's flat. He could see a light on in her window and he fingered his blackjack in his pocket. Flare sat a few tables away. He caught the reflection of the burned side of his face in the pint glass as he raised it to his lips and he clenched his fist.

White got up and left and Flare walked out into the night after him. He was entering Barlow Road when Flare hit him from behind, knocking him to the ground. White looked up to see the man he wanted dead kicking him in the face. Flare's shoe connected with bone and a crack was heard.

Just then a car drove by and Flare stopped. White scrambled to his feet and ran, thinking he didn't want him to see him enter his house. Flare lost him on Steyne Road. White kept running into the night.

33

That night as Gertrude left her flat she didn't see the Mercedes follow her all the way home.
After White got away from Flare he went to hospital to get his face fixed. Flare had broken his cheekbone. When he returned he drove to the nearest shop to buy some vodka. Driving back he saw Gertrude leave her flat and get into her car. He followed her to Gloss Road and watched her enter her house.

Lucinda Hereford sat at home waiting for Max to return from work.

She'd felt distinctly uneasy ever since the call from the police. She prepared some dinner for him, not wishing to mix with friends tonight. Chateaubriand usually went down well and she poured herself a glass of Bollinger. By the time he got in, she'd drunk most of it and he entered amused to see her wobble at the doorway.

'Busy day?', she said.

'You know.'

She ushered him inside.

'Did you hear about Jack?', he said, removing his jacket.

'Jack?', she said distantly, disappearing into the kitchen.

'Yes. He was arrested. To do with the murders. You know, Martha and her old man.'

'What could he possibly have to do with that?'

'I can't imagine. Here, let me help.'

He took the bottle from her and popped the cork.

'You're getting through a lot of champagne dear.'

'So what about Jack?'

'I don't know, that's all I heard.'

'How awful for him.'

'Well, the police must think there's some connection.'

'You know what they're like.'

'Yes, they usually get it wrong.'

Don Harvard was reading through his notes on the killings. He looked at the wound shots, zoning in on the cut marks, tracking them along the bodies. He flipped through Norris's report to see if there were any comments about this.

The next morning at the station he mentioned it.

'There's something in the way he's cutting them.'

'What?', Flare said.

'I'm not sure, but there's a distinctive style to the incisions, as if he's done it before.'

'You mean he's killed before?'

'I'm thinking more that he's used to using a knife.'

'So we're looking for a doctor or a butcher?'

'I think it's unlikely he's a surgeon, most of the cutting's too crude.'

'He could be hiding it.'

'Not that well if he was highly trained.'

'Then what?'

'There are many areas he may have worked in.'

'Like an abattoir?'

'Could be.'

'OK, so we check the work records of those involved in butchery, abattoir work, med students who dropped out, people who've produced an unusually high number of hits on websites dealing with surgical equipment.'

After Harvard left Steele felt Flare's eyes on her. Eventually she locked gazes with him and he said, 'How did you get that mark on your face?'

She swallowed at her fragmented recollection of the night with Vic. She'd spent an hour cleaning his blood off the hallway carpet and hadn't seen him since.

'I was drunk and walked into a cupboard', she said.

She went out to the ladies and found them locked. She peeked into the men's and went inside to use a cubicle. As she opened the door to one she saw Maurice Ray zipping up his trousers.

'What are you doing in here?', he said.

'You shy?'

'I'm gay.'

'I think you like women.'

'Would you get out of my way please?'

'You like me don't you?', Steele said.

'I like men.'

'Do you hate women?'

Maurice Ray's eyes veiled over as she stood there and she noticed they were dark brown. She moved her face to within inches of his and saw the outline of contact lenses in them. Then she stood back and watched him leave. She went into the next cubicle and returned to the office, glancing at Flare's wound as she walked in.

34

Gertrude saw White from the window. He stood in the street and looked up.

She didn't answer the door when he rang the bell and waited an hour before she ventured downstairs. As she drove to the shops she saw him behind her. She detoured to a road at the edge of an industrial landscape. White was right behind her when she slammed on the brakes and got out of her car.

He was getting out of his as she reached into her coat pocket.

'So, you work for me or pack up', he said.

He didn't know what it was Gertrude had in her hand as she stabbed him with it. He reached out to grab her but the skewer had punctured his heart.

White fell to his knees, pooling blood, as Gertrude got in her car and drove away. His body was found a few minutes later by a couple of teenagers who called the police.

The jars were arranged in neat rows on a steel shelf above the kitchen work surface. He stood before the metal counter holding one. It was cold to the touch and had a look of sterility to it. Dressed in white he performed an elaborate ritual, opening and turning the jars as he held them to the light. Beneath their glass were organs and skin hanging in liquid like foetuses.

He removed one and placed it on the board and got his knife and stood there feeling its sharpness in his hand.

35

Ben watched Gertrude prepare dinner the night after she killed Harlan White. He rarely thought about her outside her role as wife, but worry had started to worm its way into his mind. Ever since he'd returned from business there was something different about her and he couldn't put his finger on it.

'What are we having?', he said, inhaling the pungent odour that rose from the crackling pan.

There was a pause as she registered that he'd spoken, then she turned round.

'Fish.'

'Gertrude?'

'Yes.'

'Are you all right?'

'Yes. Why shouldn't I be?'

'You seem - troubled.'

'Troubled?'

'Yes.'

'Oh, I know what this is about.'

'Do you?'

'Sex. That's what you've got on your mind again isn't it? What is wrong with you Ben Miller?'

'This has nothing to do with sex.'

She glared at him and threw the tea towel down before marching out of the kitchen.

The tables are set,
The group has gathered.

36

Flare told Harvard about their interview with Martins.

'You're wasting your time, Jackson.'

'We've got to follow every lead at our disposal. Have you got something better?'

'Yes, as a matter of fact, I have.' Harvard paused and looked at him. Steele could see the tension building in her partner's face. 'I know you resent any challenge to your alpha male superiority', Harvard said.

'That is not what this is about.'

'Oh I think it is.'

'You psychologists think you've got it all sewn up, don't you? You think because you've passed a few exams and know a few things about your subject it gives you some divine insight into other people.'

'No.'

'Well, let me tell you, you don't have it. No one does. We have different methods, that's all, and with a little luck they can come together and maybe speed up a case. But you don't know me, you can't read me and let me tell you, there's plenty of insights any cop has that a psychologist lacks.'

'Finished?'

'No. I'm running this investigation and you're here as an aid.'

'Yes.'

'While I appreciate your input, I'm not going to have you question my methods. We interviewed Martins because that's the best we've got right now and you haven't come up with anything better, all you've brought to the table is a bunch of theories which haven't taken us a step closer to catching this guy, who's still out there.'

'You're dealing with an extreme psychopath.'

'I know. Who is leaving no forensic information at the crime scenes.'

'You're not going to solve it that quickly.'

'And you're not speeding it up.'

'Jackson, you belong to the old school.'

'Don't give me all that.'

'And it must be hard adapting to modern methods of policing.'

'I do this job to solve crimes.'

'Yes, and I do this job to help you.'

'Then help.'

'That's why I'm here.'

'Our searches for criminals with high hits on sites selling surgical equipment has led us nowhere. That's why I say we put pressure on the set of people the killer is targeting. If there's anyone in the circle the Fornalskis moved in who knows something about the killer, then by arresting Martins we may stir things up.'

'The killer is not known to them', Harvard said.

'How do you know?'

'Let me tell you. The way to catch this killer is not through looking at the circle that surrounds his victims, it's by analysing the methods he uses to kill.'

'Why don't we do both?', Flare said.

'You can.'

'We'll see what my approach produces and whether yours brings us any closer.'

'A competition?'

'No. A way of ensuring we're doing everything possible to catch this guy. The public will start to get angry very soon, this is not about showing off your latest theory, it's about bringing a murderer to justice.'

'You pursue your own line, but listen to me. This man is involved in removing body parts for a purpose and I believe he will remove more and more. Which means he will spend longer at each crime scene.'

'What does he want them for?'

'He's reconstructing himself.'

When Ben got home from work that evening he found Gertrude upstairs standing at the window. He'd come in quietly and she hadn't heard him and he stood in the semi-darkness watching her peer from behind the curtain into the street below.

'Gertrude?'

She turned and he saw anger written across her face, an unfamiliar sight. As he put the light on it fell beneath a mask.

'Turn it off!'

'What are you doing standing in the dark?'

'I thought I saw someone out there.'

'Who?'

'A man.'

Ben walked over to the window and looked into the street.

'There's no one there.'

'Not now.'

'Gertrude what's wrong?'

'I told you.'

'Something's been wrong with you for days.'

'No.'

He tried to reach for her hand but she marched off and went downstairs where she began preparing dinner.

WORKING THE WIVES

37

It wasn't long before news that Harlan White had been killed reached Flare. He raised a query that it was to do with the case. White's body was transported to the pathology lab at his station. Frank Norris took them through what he had.

'He was stabbed straight through the heart with a long sharp instrument', Norris said.

'Any idea what the weapon was?', Flare said.

'I think it was a skewer.'

'Who would walk around with that on them?'

White lay there like a slab of menace, his heart opened and his face closed. Flare thought back to the night he assaulted him, of how he wanted to kill him.

'He also has other injuries', Norris said. 'His nose was recently broken and his cheekbone is broken.'

'Are they separate to the murder?'

'Yes, the first injury is some weeks old, the second fresh, but he had been treated for it before he was killed.'

'I don't know what to make of this. Whether someone tried more than once to kill him.'

'It's possible the injuries were sustained as a result of provocation on White's part. The person who killed him may not have intended to do so.'

'One thing's for sure, White had enemies.'

Throughout the examination Steele said nothing.

When they returned to the office Flare said 'Is everything OK?'

'I've seen that man before.'

'Harlan White?'

'Is he the man you burnt?'

'He is. He was a serial rapist, he did some terrible things to the prostitutes whose lives he took away.'

'I believe you.'

'How did you know him?'

'A few weeks ago I was attacked by him.'

'Attacked?'

'He dragged me into an alley and tried to rape me.'

'Why didn't your report this?'

'I got away, it would have been impossible finding him.'

'You fought him off.'

'I broke his nose.'

'Good for you.'

'He tried to rape me with a blackjack, he didn't succeed.'

'I'll tell you something. I started thinking about White again when this case started. I tracked him down. A few nights ago I assaulted him.'

'What did you do?'

'I broke his cheekbone.'

'So who killed him?'

'That I don't know, but one thing's for sure, it's not our killer.'

38

Dressed immaculately in an Alberta Ferretti skirt and blouse, Lucinda Hereford waited nervously in the lobby of The Lowndes.

She drank two Martinis in quick succession and glanced sharply at her watch, irritated at Jack's lateness. As she tried to settle on an ultimatum with which to issue him she looked out of the window and saw his Jaguar draw up. She was standing at the passenger door before he switched off his mobile.

'Talking to another one of your ladies?' she said.

'Talking to my bank manager darling. Drink?'

'Had one. Had two', she said, getting in. 'I'm glad I went to deportment classes, in this skirt I could be showing more than a lady would like to.'

'Where are we going?'

'How about your flat?'

Inside he poured them both a glass of wine, cool and white from Languedoc. As he had his back turned to her, Lucinda loosened her blouse, checking her cleavage in the huge mirror that covered almost an entire wall.

Jack handed her a glass.

'Hot?', he said.

'Worried.'

'You, worried?'

'Max heard.'

'Heard what?'

'Oh come on Jack, about you being arrested.'

'And?'

'Max always thinks there's no smoke without fire, I know him, he'll get suspicious.'

'Of what? Me screwing his delicious wife?'

'Why did they arrest you?'

'Bloody police, they've got nothing better to do.'

'Seriously.'

'They're digging, that's all they know how to do.'

'And is there anything to dig up on you?'

'Apart from the fact that you enjoy my company, no. And they won't tell Max.'

'So, don't worry?'

'Never worry, Lucinda, it spoils your face.'

He reached his arm round her waist. For a moment she pulled away before putting her glass down and setting her mouth firmly on his and falling backwards onto his bed.

He undressed her slowly, placing a kiss on every inch of her skin as he unveiled her. He placed his mouth fully on hers and she dissolved.

Afterwards, when he was in the shower she went through his drawers looking for evidence of other women, only to find a doctor's letter from a private surgery diagnosing venereal disease.

Michael McKleith checked himself in the mirror.

The hard lines of his face circled his eyes, his skin was thickened from all the fights he'd been in. He was hard to put down. Many men had tried but he always got back up.

Pale sunlight leaked into the dirty street below. An old man walked slowly past the window, ushering in memories of his father.

Known locally in the East End where he grew up as Gobstopper Harry, he'd often beat a man near to death if he said something he didn't like.

McKleith remembered once, aged eight, when his father took him for a walk. This usually involved stopping at a pub while he left him outside. On this occasion, Michael poked his head inside to see where his father had got to.

He sat among his friends drinking and joking. One of them saw Michael there and said, 'Your son's after you.'

'Get back out there', Harry said.

Michael did as he was told, but as he turned he heard someone say 'Always bring the nipper with you? What kind of a man are you, where's your missus?'

'What did you say?'

Harry turned round on his stool.

Michael watched from the edge of the door as the other man stood up. He was large and well built.

'You're just a show boat. Sitting there lording it over the pub. I said where's the missus? That's a woman's job, you bringing a boy here and leaving him alone, what kind of father are you?'

Harry squared up to him. He was shorter than him but better muscled. Michael knew what was coming. He'd seen it often enough.

They stood facing each other for a few moments before the other guy threw the first punch. Harry blocked it and hit him so hard in the stomach he doubled him over, then he brought his knee up into his face and Michael heard the crunch of breaking bone. Blood spurted from his nose and Harry swept his legs from under him, kicking him until he wasn't moving. His drinking mates applauded him and dragged the guy out into the car park where they left him. The landlord was among them.

Harry then walked Michael to the shops talking about football. Michael would never forget what happened next. He often said his father made him who he was.

Michael was short for his age. He grew a lot later, but he was being picked on at school at that time, a fact he hid from his father because he knew what he would do if he found out.

Harry left Michael in the street while he chatted to the newsagent and as he stood there Tom and Wally walked by. They were two hard kids who'd beaten up most of his year. Tom was the ringleader but you wouldn't have wanted to get on the wrong side of Wally.

'What you looking at?', Tom said.

'Nothing.'

'You are.'

They stopped and stared him down.

'Little runt', Wally said.

He threw a punch and it smacked Michael in the side of the face and he ran away down the street.

Harry was walking out of the shop with his copy of The Star and saw this. He stood in the doorway and making eye contact with his son, summoned him with his finger.

Tom and Wally started to move off down the road as Michael approached cautiously.

'What you doing?', Harry said.

'Nothing.'

'No you weren't. I saw that, you don't stand for that do you hear me? Now you know what you're going to do?' Michael looked away. 'Look at me. What're you going to do?'

'I'll deal with them.'

'Now.'

'Dad.'

'Now.'

Michael stood there, hoping the boys would disappear, but they waited at the corner of the road laughing at him.

'Are you going to let them take the piss of you? No son of mine's going to get pushed around. You go and teach them a lesson. If you don't, I'll teach you a lesson. Now, who are you more frightened of, them or me?'

'You.'

'Good. So show them they never do that to you again, understand?'

With his heart beating like a hammer in his chest Michael walked slowly to where they stood, their laughter ringing in his ears. His mouth felt dry, his legs were hollow, and his hands were sweating when he got to them.

'What do you want?', Tom said.

'Don't do that again', Michael said.

'What?'

'I'm not going to take it anymore.'

Tom started laughing and Michael lashed out.

The first punch was wild and landed on his cheek, rousing him into a look of startled anger. He hadn't hurt him and Wally grabbed Michael's arms while Tom hit him hard in the face. Harry watched without moving from his spot. Then Michael heard him.

'Michael!'

And something uncoiled inside him.

He kicked Wally, shaking him off, and then smacked Tom so hard in the face his lip broke across his mouth. He pushed him over and jumped on him, kicking his head until it was swollen.

Wally just stood there until Michael turned round, when he threw a weak punch which Michael ducked. Coming up he connected beautifully with his jaw and watched Wally fall backwards. He hit him repeatedly on the nose, connecting again and again with it until there was no nose on his face and he lay without moving next to his mate.

He wanted to do more but Harry came and pulled him off.

'That's better', he said. He looked at Michael. 'Good. You got it. That's my boy. Now remember that's what you do next time anyone gives you any grief. Got it?'

'Yes, dad.'

They returned home where his mother was making their lunch. As they sat down to eat he watched his father's face behind The Star. He could still feel the hard thing that had opened inside him when he began hitting Tom and Wally. It sat inside him like metal and he wondered what it was. Now, years later, Michael knew the answer, it was the road of his violent future opening before him.

The old man disappeared at the end of the road and Michael stared again at his tired face in the mirror.

He remembered the incident in prison with the screw who'd aggravated him. He kicked him so hard his shoe lodged in the guard's cheek. Pulling it away yanked some tissue with it and Michael heard the squelch of skin and vein beneath his feet as he walked away.

The memories of his father and mother faded in his mind like the steam from his breath against the mirror.

He thought of his life before prison, before he beat the police officer so badly he was forced to retire. And the daughter he'd never seen again. He remembered the fleeting face of a frightened girl and wondered where his wife was now.

Then he turned to the cupboard in the bare room and removed the Luger from the drawer at the bottom and began putting the bullets in the chamber.

39

They do not hold the mirror
I do.

At home Lucinda was talking to Mirabelle on the phone.

'He's just too good to resist that's why I did it.'

'I know he's a peach, darling, but right under Max's nose, you've got front.'

Lucinda popped the cork on the chilled Pouilly Fuisse she was holding, looking at the clock, thinking noon was fine, under the circumstances.

'Do you think he suspects?', Mirabelle said.

'Who, Max?'

'Yes.'

'No.'

'He's not playing games, is he?'

'I'm sure he doesn't suspect', Lucinda said.

'He's not stupid and the way he keeps talking about Jack's arrest could be a way of seeing your reaction.'

'You think?'

'Yes.'

Lucinda watched the drops run down the side of the bottle.

'Well, he's a fine one to talk.'

'You mean after his, what shall I call it?'

'Affair, call it a bloody affair.'

'Men who do it are most prone to jealousy.'

'That's true.'

'And you don't think he suspects?'

'No.'

'Then what are you worried about?'

'It's Jack.'

'What about him?'

'The other day when I was at his flat I saw something.'

'What?'

'I don't know whether I should even be saying this.'

'For God's sake, Lucinda, what was it, a head in the fridge?'

'OK, OK, I'll tell you.'

She took a swig of wine.

'Yes?'

'He's got syphilis.'

'What?'

'I saw a letter from the clinic.'

'Are you sure?'

'It was at his flat, it said J Martin on it.'

'He's being treated then.'

'Well, yes.'

'Get yourself checked out, you don't want to pass it on to Max, because then he really will know what you've been up to.'

'You're right.'

'I know a doctor.'

'I can't believe he wouldn't tell me.'

'I can.'
'What else don't I know about Jack?'
'I'll give you the name of my doctor.'

40

Ben sat down and stared at the brown and red mixture congealing at the edge of his plate.

He'd seen the worried look etched into his children's faces as he entered the kitchen and he glanced furtively at Gertrude, who avoided eye contact and stood scouring a pan prematurely.

'You usually do that afterwards', he said.

'Just eat.'

He set fork to plate and paused, wondering what he was looking at.

The meat was gelatinous, globular, and small veins threaded away from its ribboned sides.

'Gertrude?'

'Yes.'

Her voice was far away and she stood scraping and rubbing the pan repeatedly, lost in the motion. It reminded him of inmates of asylums who rock repeatedly back and forth.

'What is this?'

'What is what?'

'The dinner.'

'Stew.'

'What sort of stew?'

'Meat.'

He picked a piece up, watching Maxwell avoid his and concentrate on his vegetables, while Mary pushed hers around her plate nervously. He held it to the light. It was grey and its centre was a marbleised red. He set it in his mouth and chewed. It tasted like chicken, and he soon dismissed his anxiety as neurosis, eating most of it.

Gertrude didn't join them. She stood with her back to them washing up. When they'd finished she took their plates from them without a word.

Ben went into the living room with the kids who watched TV while he read the paper.

They went upstairs later and Gertrude came through and sat next to him knitting. After a while he found the interminable clicking of her needles infuriating and he looked at her until she stopped.

'Everything all right dear?' she said.

'No, it's not.'

'Dinner not right?'

'No, it was fine, a little unusual, maybe, but fine.'

'What then?'

'Could you stop that for a minute?'

She looked at him, unaware of what he was referring to and then looked down at her needles and set them to one side.

'So what is the matter?'

'I'm worried about you.'

'Worried about me?'

'I've been worried about you for weeks.'

'For heaven's sake, why?'

'There's something wrong.'

'Nothing's wrong.'

'There is, with you', he said with alarm creeping into his voice now.

'I'm fine dear.'

And she picked up her needles and started knitting again. Ben sat there in silence for a while before trying to engage her in conversation.

'It says in the paper they still aren't any closer to catching the serial killer.'

'Oh?'

'You know, the one who's been mutilating bodies.'

'Disgusting.'

'He's going around cutting people up and the police haven't got the faintest clue who he is.'

She put her needles down.

'I know what the matter with you is.'

'The matter with me?'

'Sex. It's all right, we can go to bed early tonight.'

And she left the room.

Ben sat there considering her comment and decided that perhaps he could get her to talk to him this way and find out what was bothering her.

Once the kids were asleep he went up to the darkened room carrying the tea she'd made him and lay down next to her.

He reached out a hand and touched her.

She felt cold.

He touched her bottom and she winced.

'What is it?'

'Nothing.'

He felt very tired and didn't wake until the next morning when Gertrude had already risen.

41

Mirabelle's doctor, Stuart Johnson, was a Harley Street specialist in venereal disease used to treating wealthy ladies who wanted discreet consultations in conducive surroundings. He was handsome, toned, and used just enough charm not to overstep his professional boundaries.

Lucinda had never been to a venereal specialist before and felt sick and angry with Jack for putting her through this. As she sat reading Tattler she thought how she couldn't even discuss it with him and that made her feel lower. She could never admit to snooping. If she had contracted syphilis then she could talk to him. And how.

As Stuart Johnson conducted her into his room she relaxed and almost forgot why she was there. She explained the situation, glancing at the calming Rothkos on the wall, wondering whether they were prints, before going into the bathroom where she undressed behind the curtain.

Dr. Johnson asked the usual diagnostic questions as he examined her. She began to feel angry with Jack again.

'You show no signs of infection, so if you have

contracted something it's in its early stages, which is good news, Mrs. Hereford, because it is easily treated. I'll take a blood test.'

When she stood up she noticed her legs were shaking. She paid at reception and drove home. She hadn't spoken to Jack since she ran out of his flat. He'd since left a message which she ignored. She sat down to think what she would tell Max if the news was bad.

Gertrude stopped outside the brightly polished windows of the shop. She hadn't noticed it before: a Gentleman's Outfitter. It seemed a little incongruous in the backwaters of suburbia, tucked away as it was between the chemist and fishmonger. She thought of Burlington Arcade, and the expensive rows of stores that lined central London.

She liked the name: Clean Shave, and she gazed at the products that had been carefully placed in the window. Razors, shaving brushes, travel boxes and powders. She felt transported back to another time, an older time when people behaved differently, when they knew where they stood and manners were the order of the day.

The image of a man standing before a large mirror with his face lathered flashed into her mind and she moved forward instinctively. The bell rang at the door, rousing her from her reverie.

'Can I help, Madam?', the shopkeeper said.

He had an old fashioned face and didn't seem to fit

in the present era. Gertrude felt charmed and young again.

'Yes, I want to buy a present.'

'For your husband?'

'That's right.'

'Well, we have some lovely products Madam, does he wet shave?'

'Always.'

'You'd be surprised how many people use electric razors these days, but they never achieve the desired effect, leaving bits of stubble sticking out at most unfortunate angles. If you saw some of the shaves I've witnessed carried out by the best products on the market, well, you'd know what I'm talking about, but with these, with any of these your husband will achieve the closest shave possible, like a professional job.'

'I see.'

'Now, do you know what make your husband presently uses?'

'I'm afraid not.'

'That doesn't matter, let me show you some of our products. Many of these are handmade.'

She looked at the range he set before her.

'Now, this is our cheapest model, a Nickel finish Butterfly razor. It gives a close shave and accompanying it, a good quality brush and some cream. Working our way upwards, you can see just by looking how the quality differs, going right through to the top of the range.'

'I like the old fashioned method', Gertrude said,

looking at the shop owner's face, searching for stubble, or signs of nicks.

'I see, you mean the Cut Throat razor. That is indeed the finest way', the shopkeeper said, leaning into her and lowering his voice, 'some would say the only way to achieve a perfect shave.'

'That is what I want for my husband', Gertrude said, 'the elimination of all hair.'

'Then this is the one to buy him', he said, pointing to a razor that lay open on invitingly black velvet. 'This has a mother of pearl handle with a 6/8" blade.'

He picked it up and handed it to her.

Gertrude touched the edge.

'Careful Madam', the shopkeeper said. 'It's very fine.'

'I never cut myself by accident.'

'It's made by the finest craftsmen and lasts a lifetime, also I would recommend a pure badger shaving brush.'

He passed her one and she ran her hand along its bristles.

'You can feel the quality.'

'Yes, I can.'

'Will you be taking the Cut Throat and the badger?'

'I will.'

'An excellent choice madam, he won't be disappointed. Men have said their lives have been changed by a razor. Shall I add a fine cream?'

'Yes.' She watched as he packed them into a box. 'It's strange finding you here, a shop like this is normally in central London', she said.

The shopkeeper looked at her for a moment and

Gertrude was about to apologise for the remark when he said, 'There is always the need for a good razor Madam.'

'Do you think I could buy some of those blades as well?', she said, pointing to a shelf behind him.

'You mean the safety razor blades?'

'Yes.'

'He won't need them with this.'

'No, it's for someone else.'

'I see, yes of course, shall I put them in the same bag?'

'That would be fine.'

'That will be £260 Madam.'

She paid and left the shop.

As she walked away she heard an incessant scraping noise. It sounded like sandpaper on stone and she couldn't drive the sound from her head.

Back at home she put the bag on the side and removed the safety blades. She walked upstairs and took her clothes off and stood before the bathroom mirror. Finding a section of flesh at her side she began to peel away her skin.

ZOOM LENS

42

Michael McKleith knew it would still be there.

The abandoned Ford with the expired tax disc sat in the empty street near the post office. McKleith lifted the hanger out of his bag, nudged it down inside the window, and found the lock. He got in and hotwired it, stopping at the first garage he came to and putting in just enough petrol for the job. He parked some distance from the boarding house and went inside to fetch what he needed, trying the balaclava on before he left.

On the way he stopped in a quiet street to buy some Marlboros. He had to wait for the newsagent to serve him because he was talking on the phone and McKleith looked at him in irritation, curbing his anger to harness it for what he was about to do. When he got outside he found a traffic warden issuing him with a ticket.

'What do you think you're doing?', McKleth said.

'You're illegally parked Sir.'

'I only went in for these.'

He waved the cigarettes at him.

'This is a parking offence.'

'I was gone for a minute.'

The warden ignored him and McKleith looked

around. There was no one to be seen. He punched the warden in the side of the face, knocking him to the ground.

The warden stared up at him in disbelief as McKleith kicked him again and again, driving the blood from him, scraping the skin from his face. The warden held his hands up to protect himself, but McKleith kept on with the assault until he wasn't moving and then he drove away.

Anne Lacey got back late after a long shoot.

As she stepped across the threshold of her bedroom she felt a hand against her face before she passed out.

She awoke to see a figure standing over her and she screamed.

He silenced her with his gloved hand and she stared at him, searching for his face behind his mask.

'You were always so decorative, you little flirt. How many men have stared at your body?', he said. 'I see you've been on a Fendi shoot. Click click. They have shot after shot of you, but the picture I'm going to take of you in your final hour will be worth more than all of them put together. Let me remove these clothes from you so I may do what I want with your body, use you like the whore you are and take away the thing I have come here for. Stare at me with those green eyes Anne, soon the light will be gone from them. I will take it with me and a piece of you. Oh your skin is soft, don't wriggle, I'm just going to pull your panties off, that's it, I see you have a sliced peach between your legs, nice and appealing, I bet it tastes good too. You like your amoretto don't you? You like them seeing you beneath the soft rustling see-through silk you wear, while behind your mask you watch desire creep into them.'

Anne struggled but the killer's arms were too strong and she began to lose consciousness as he pinned her to the floor, cutting away her clothes. Then he removed a long knife from his bag and began to open her from her crutch to her neck. He stood back and took two pictures in quick succession with his S2 Leica. He got a pair of scissors and cut her luxuriant blonde hair until she was almost bald. He shaved the rest off with an electric razor. He took some flesh from her. Then he cut the letter S into her neck.

Her body was found by her cleaner the next morning. She was lying on her bed, her intestines coiled about her like snakes. The cleaner vomited before she reached the phone and when the police arrived they found her cleaning up her own sick.

43

As Flare and Steele made their way to Anne Lacey's flat they knew she was another victim in the case. What they saw confirmed it.

Al Groper, Maurice Ray's colleague, was gathering evidence.

'Where's Maurice?', Flare said.

'I don't know', Groper said.

Steele walked over to the body.

'He's opened her right up', she said.

'I wonder if she was sexually abused.'

'Like Don said, he's taking more and more away.'

'Let's find out as much as we can about her and whether she was connected in any way to the others', Flare said.

Michael McKleith sat in his room rethinking his plans after the incident with the warden.

There were plenty of other cars.

He left and toured the streets, passing into the backwaters of the surrounding area until he found one. An abandoned Vauxhall Vectra, it would do, fast enough and anonymous. He drove straight there, sticking to the speed limit all the way, watchful of cameras and on the lookout for cops. The Luger lay in his pocket like a friend. He thought about how he only had enough money for two more packs of cigarettes and felt angry.

Stopping a few streets away he got out. He walked to the post office, glancing through the door. It was twelve o'clock and there was only one customer inside.

He walked down the side alley and stood behind the dustbins where he donned his balaclava before returning to the empty shop. He shut the door and locked it.

'Hey what do you think you're doing?', the owner said.

McKleith walked up to him.

'Where's your assistant?'

'In the store room.'

'Get him!'

The man hesitated and McKleith pointed the gun at him.

He called out a name and a young man came out of the door at the side. 'Stay there', McKleith said, pushing his way past him into the office. He could see the owner was shaking.

'Money', McKleith said.

'It's in the safe.'

'Get it!'

He opened the safe and McKleith began taking the cash out, which he placed in his holdall. Then he struck the owner across the back of the head, knocking him to the floor. He walked round to where the young man stood and pistol whipped him until he was down and left the shop.

As he walked away he didn't see the old man walk in. He saw the injured shopkeeper and raised the alarm. Two police officers were coming round the corner when they heard him shouting. They ran to him and ascertained what had happened.

'Did you see which way he went?', one of the officers said.

The old man pointed at the road McKleith had walked towards. The officers raced there, the younger of the two making ground while the other officer caught his foot on an upturned paving stone. He crashed to the ground and saw his colleague disappear at the end of the road.

McKleith was getting into his car. A van was blocking the road and he began to turn the Vauxhall round. It stalled. McKleith started swearing, seeing the policeman running towards him. As he switched the ignition on again and the engine kicked into life the officer opened the door and started to pull him out, grabbing the bag.

McKleith punched him, knocking him over. He got out and the officer struck him twice before McKleith began in earnest. He smashed his cheek in with the pistol.

The officer was on the ground and McKleith placed his foot against his neck, pushing until a loud crack was heard. Then he shot him twice in the head and drove away, dumping the car some distance from the boarding house.

In his room he showered and checked out.

44

The eyes of a pit viper and the mouth of an angel
Perhaps Razor will remember her like that.

They pulled Razor in for questioning. Among the contents of Anne Lacey's Vivienne Westwood handbag was a photograph of her injuries. She'd written 'What Razor did to me' on the back.

It didn't take Flare and Steele long to find out he'd been accused of assaulting Anne, and they dragged him, very angry and very hung over into the station. Steele could see Flare itching to get to him. As he strode down the corridor to the interview room she said, 'OK, you're the bad cop, how do you want me to play this?'

'The other bad cop.'

Razor sat there looking jumpy.

'You like beating up women don't you?', Flare said.

'That's the tabloids.'

'So you didn't assault Anne Lacey before killing her?'

Steele could hear the alarm creep into Razor's voice as he answered.

'I didn't kill anyone.'

'You beat her up pretty badly.'

'That's bullshit.'

'Is this bullshit?', Flare said, laying the picture on the table in front of him.

Reality broke across Razor's numb face.

'Make it easy on yourself', Steele said, 'tell us what happened and we may go easy on you.'

'We had an argument, that's all, yeah I hit her, I was coked out of my head, but I never killed her.'

Flare leaned back and folded his arms.

'And you expect us to believe that?'

'Yeah.'

'Not good enough.'

'I haven't seen her since it happened. Anne had problems, she was into coke like you wouldn't believe and she was always whoring around.'

'Well, someone killed her in a very nasty fashion.'

'What?'

'Someone removed her intestines.'

'No shit?'

'You were spotted parked outside her flat by a neighbour.'

'I went round there, I didn't even get to see her.'

'No?'

'I passed out. I was asleep and when I woke up I drove away.'

'This doesn't sound too good, Razor.'

45

There was no adequate description of McKleith, since the other officer hadn't seen him and the old man's memory was already growing faint.

Meanwhile from his hotel room in central London McKleith rang an old friend.

'Hello, Archie? It's Michael. I'm out. A few weeks. It feels good. Yes, Archie, and how are things? There's a favour I have to ask. I need you to find someone for me. I can pay.'

So filthy and so young,
Soiled beyond belief.
Her best commodity was tucked away
Within the folds of her skin.

Ben wondered why Gertrude had bought him a new shaving kit. He tried using it and was impressed by its quality, even if he held the Cut Throat razor nervously.

'It must have cost a bit', he said, feeling his chin after using it.

'He said it would give a good shave.'

'It does. What's the occasion?'

'Do I need an occasion?'

'No.'

'It's just a little out of character.'

'Is it?'

'Yes.'

'Do you really think there's such a thing as character?'

He watched as she walked away, wondering where his wife had gone, seeing the shadow of Gertrude somewhere between him and this other woman who spoke in riddles. He searched for Gertrude in the conversations that fell like lost coins in the space between them.

46

'She was not sexually assaulted', Frank Norris said, as he took Flare and Steele through the wounds inflicted on Anne Lacey. 'The killer severed her vagina and ran his knife up to her neck, he butchered her.'

'Has he removed any organs?', Flare said.

'He removed her breasts. As with the other victims, she has a letter carved into her neck, and there's something else we haven't seen before.'

Norris raised one eyelid with a pair of surgical pliers.

'What is that, some sort of contact lens?', Steele said.

'It's a camera lens from a Hammacher Schlemmer camera, the world's smallest camera. He has done the same thing to both her eyes.'

'You're saying he's removed the camera lenses and placed them in her eyes?', Flare said.

'I am. The camera itself is only an inch in all dimensions.'

Paul and Samantha DeLonge sat in their enormous dining room having breakfast.

Their Phillipino maid studiously set cutlery and plates beside them while Samantha stared at Paul, searching his face behind the Financial Times. From time to time she let out a tired sigh which he ignored.

Eventually he set the paper down, folding it neatly and placing it to his left where he could still scan the article he was reading about commodities.

'Did you hear about Jack Martins?', Samantha said.

'I heard the little creep was arrested.'

Paul munched absent-mindedly on some toast.

'Creep?'

'Yes.'

'I didn't realise you disliked him.'

He turned to look at her and she felt he was searching her face.

'I think he's a philandering aging gigolo who spends too much time hanging round other men's wives, I think he's untrustworthy and has never done an honest day's work in his life.'

'They say he's been having an affair.'

'That doesn't surprise me.'

'With Lucinda.'

'Lucinda?'

'Yes.'

'She must be mad.'

'I think she's mad now.'

'Why was he arrested?'

'Something to do with these killings.'

'He's not a killer.'

'He did have an affair with Martha Fornalski.'

'So long as he hasn't been having one with you.'

'Don't be ridiculous.'

'I've seen the way he looks at you.'

'I only have eyes for you darling.'

'Well, let it stay that way.'

'He's obviously been a bad boy, done something the police have on him for them to arrest him like that in front of the whole golf club.'

'Wouldn't surprise me, but I don't think it's murder.'

'No.'

'Does Max know?'

'I don't believe he does.'

Paul picked his paper up.

'At least now he has the reputation he deserves.'

'Which is what?', Samantha said.

'A bad one.'

She sat there watching him read, while behind him the green lawns of their house stretched away to nothingness.

'Paul?'

'Yes.'

'You won't tell Max, will you?'

'Tell him what?'

'I know he's a good friend of yours, but it would destroy him, it would destroy their marriage.'

He looked at her over the pink border of the FT.

'I think he deserves to know.'

Her thoughts were momentarily distracted by the headline 'World Stock Markets Crumble'. She thought about their money vanishing, their lifestyle being threatened, and she shivered. The idea of being outside her exclusive club was unbearable, and she rallied herself.

'Don't tell him.'

'Well, I might.'

'Why?'

'Because he has a right to know.'

'Think of the effect it would have, think of Lucinda, she has no future with Jack now, everyone would spurn her if she went back to him.'

'She shouldn't have done it then.'

'Paul.'

'Why did you tell me?'

'You're my husband.'

'Do you tell me everything?'

'Yes.'

'Oh come on.'

'I don't have any secrets.'

'I don't mean that, do you tell me every bit of tittle tattle you and your friends discuss?'

'Well, no.'

'So then.'

'This is different.'

'And Max is my friend.'

'I know.'

'Who told you?'

'Mirabelle.'

'That old gossip.'

'Paul.'

'Well, she is.'

'What are you going to do?'

'I don't know, I'm going to think about it. Anyway, I thought you and Mirabelle didn't talk anymore.'

'Who told you that?'

'Lucinda.'

'We had a disagreement, but it's all over now.'

He turned to his paper again and she left the room.

Outside the maid was cleaning the hallway and Samantha passed by her, ascending the stairs gracefully.

In her bedroom she smoothed her hair before the mirror and then opened a small drawer.

Taking a key from her purse she unlocked a compartment at its back and removed some letters. Next to them lay Jack's picture.

Later that day Flare and Steele met with Don Harvard.

'What do you make of this one?', Flare said.

'There is more attention in the way he's killing the women than the men. He smashes a bottle of Hermes perfume when he kills Martha Fornalski, he hangs Sandra Gould with a rope. Now he shaves a model's head. There is an underlying moral message, perhaps religious in origin.'

'Can we chase it up?', Flare said.

'I'll search. Removing her breasts is sexual.'

'What do you make of the camera lenses?'

'It's about watching, the killer wants to have surveillance of his victims. Anne Lacey was a model, so she was photographed a lot.'

'What about the letter S?', Steele said.

'Stephanie, it's the lingerie brand of Steph Aman, and he's got the letter just right. Each time he shapes it well, he's skilled with his hands. I would imagine you will find Anne Lacey has some Steph Aman lingerie. It's very revealing, she specialises in sheer lingerie that shows much of the female body. It's erotic and seductive. She also likes using masks with her models.'

'Masks?', Steele said.

'Yes. One of her styles is called amoretto's facade. It's about revealing the body and hiding the face. This could be a key to something that is motivating the killer.'

'What does it represent?', Flare said.

'The hidden sexual lives of his victims. Women showing so much of their bodies, hiding their identities, the killer wants access to that.'

47

The Detectives look in all the wrong places,
Two intruders in a world that does not welcome them.
It is darkened to them, they hold no map,
They are in the wrong city.

Archie called McKleith back with the information he wanted.

'I've got the address', he said.

'That was quick.'

'My man's good. Got a pen and paper?'

'Yeah.'

He wrote it down.

'Enjoy your freedom Michael.'

'I will. Thanks Archie.'

He sat looking at the address for a while before leaving his hotel room and walking past the sea of faces in the street outside.

He found a pub and sat in the corner with a whisky. He could see his past swimming up from the glass, and its acrid tang left the smear of memory in his thoughts, like a smoke mark on the wall of a room. He turned his back to the other customers and sat facing the wall.

The sun broke through the clouds and sent a ray dancing along the surface of the filthy table as something darkened in his mind.

He stared ahead, the outlines of a grimy picture swimming into view. It hung there lopsided on the wall of the pub, a portrait of a family eating, the mother serving food to a bloated girl while the father kicked a small dog under the table. A boy hung back at the doorway. McKleith's face ghosted itself into the portrait. He watched his own reflection as he lifted his glass to his lips.

He fumbled in his pocket for cigarettes, feeling a piece of paper lying there. Then he walked to the machine in the corner and bought a pack and left.

It was a hot morning when Lucinda came downstairs in her dressing gown.

She reached for the paracetamol, knocking over one of the bottles she'd left on the floor the night before. Sweat ran down the backs of her legs.

In the hall she could see the mail lying on the mat and she walked over to pick it up, stars dancing as she stood. Most of it was for Max and she put his to one side.

When she got to the envelope she knew what it was before opening it. Inside the Harley Street address stared at her as she unfolded the letter.

As she read it dread turned to reality and she opened her first bottle of the day

PLAYTHINGS

48

Anne Lacey had a lot of Steph Aman in her wardrobe. Steele looked at the luxury lingerie maker's website after Don's visit. She spent a long time staring at the beautiful, posed bodies of the women who wore 100% pure silk chiffon, their breasts visible beneath it, their faces masked. They seemed placed there for the enjoyment of men. She felt angry and aroused.

She found herself comparing her body to those of the models and she measured her desirability. She looked at Flare, at his wound, and felt able to let her eyes linger on it without the usual distaste. As she left the station that evening she realised something had changed in the way she felt about him. It was as if by discovering what he had done to Harlan White, Allen's shadow no longer lay on Flare.

Vic Jones was in the corridor as she left and she almost went back in. There was a moment when he held her in a frozen stare. Then he walked past her, still looking at her. He passed so close to her he almost touched her and he was gone.

Steele returned to her flat and called Mark, leaving a message asking him to come over.

She showered and looked at her body in the mirror.

She still had good breasts and dressed right she could pull most men. Dressed right. She thought of the victims she was seeing cut up.

Mark arrived as she was pouring her first vodka. They sat and drank.

'I want to do something different tonight', she said.

'What do you have in mind?'

'You'll see.'

'I knew you'd want it again, it's like a drug.'

Steele started to undress and watched as Mark removed his trousers and shirt. Then she went into the bathroom returning naked wearing the mask she'd bought on the way home. She saw Mark had an erection and walked over and started rubbing it.

'I can be who I want', she said.

'You can be whoever I want you to be.'

She led him to the bed and cuffed him and sat on top of him. She looked at herself in the mirror as she moved up and down, her face covered, and she felt freed to do what she wanted.

She hit him and he tried to resist but she hit harder. When she'd come she walked away and removed the mask. Her eyes were full of a satisfaction she had never seen before, not since Allen took some part of her away.

She uncuffed Mark and he began to dress.

'There are plenty of things we can do', he said.

'Desire is lawless and I know that now.'

That morning Gertrude awoke from a nightmare she couldn't shake off.

She'd tried cleaning every cupboard in the house once Mary and Maxwell had gone to school, but the feeling wouldn't go away.

She looked around at her immaculate suburban home and smelt her hands, inhaling the strong odour of bleach. But beneath it was another smell, faint as mist in the morning.

She ran a tap and rinsed away a tiny residue of tea, letting the water cascade down her hands as a fragment of the dream rolled into her mind.

A toy upon the windowsill, and a rope swinging from a large tree.

She stands and looks up into its branches.

She walks towards the house, the back door is open, there is blood on the tiles, her mother is crying.

A man stands in the hallway but she cannot see his face.

Her body feels like some weight attached to her, it is not her own.

As the images faded and the sound of running water sharpened in her mind, she managed to stem the flow of urine on her legs.

49

Away from the company of men he would sometimes talk for hours. The other stood at his elbow advising him. The image would remain there in the corner of the vast and silent room, untroubled by sound except for the lash of his whip, which he administered like some captain dealing in derangement. The grieving and quiet face was etched into his mind like a scar with acid. He sought him out in his troubled sleep, and saw him in the sallow faces of street beggars, their human isolation a fragment of his despair. And still he tortured Christ within the quiet workings of his own soul, hunting him into the abyss.

For he lay beyond sound like a mute. The turmoil was never spent and he wrangled with the dark, seeing shapes flee and forms settle within the accepted contours of reality.

When Ben returned home that evening the smell of bleach overpowered him as he walked through the door. Mary and Maxwell were upstairs and had shut themselves in their rooms to avoid the stench. He found Gertrude emptying the washing machine.

'Did you spill something?', he said.

'Don't be disgusting.'

'What's disgusting about that?'

'You know what I mean.'

'No, I don't know what you mean, the house stinks of bleach.'

'You want a clean house, don't you?'

She marched past him carrying the load of washing.

In the rubbish he saw the empty bottles of cleaning products and watched as Gertrude moved about the kitchen preparing dinner, like someone late for an appointment.

As she turned to the window she saw a tall man lathering his face at the kitchen sink. He held a razor in one hand and his eyes caught hers in the darkened window pane.

50

They held Razor until Steele had a conversation with Marigold Steer, one of Anne's neighbours. Steele was hoping to find something tangible on him, despite the unshakeable sense she had that this high-profile rock star was not their man. Marigold Steer invited her in and offered her a cup of tea, which for once she accepted, tired as she was from the long hours she'd been putting in.

'I've seen him coming and going', Marigold said.

'Who?'

'That rock star.'

'Razor?'

'Yes.'

'Have you ever heard any arguments between him and Anne?'

'Oh, I've heard arguments all right.'

'Would you say they were violent?'

'It depends how you would define violent.'

'Did you ever hear Anne crying out? Did you think she was being hit?'

'It's hard to say. But I've read what he did in the press.'

'The assault? Please tell me anything you know, as

you can see, Anne was in danger before she was killed.'

'Well, I can tell you something, but you're not going to like what it is.'

'Whatever it is, it may help the investigation.'

'It wasn't him.'

'Who? Razor?'

'Yes.'

'You're saying he didn't kill Anne?'

'Yes.'

'And why do you say that?'

'Because I saw Anne returning. I was looking out of my window. I'd seen him pull up earlier and he'd been ringing on her bell and shouting in the street. He'd been sitting in his car and when she came home he was slumped over the steering wheel. He'd been like that for hours. He'd obviously done too many drugs and passed out.'

'He could still have gone in and killed her.'

'He didn't. I saw him wake up a few minutes later and drive off, not long after she came back.'

'What time was that?'

'I remember looking at my watch. One o'clock.'

'Do you usually stand at your window for hours?'

'Not usually, but I saw her come in and I didn't leave the window until he drove away. I was concerned for her safety after reading about him in the papers and I thought if he caused trouble I'd call the police. I watched her go in and a while later he woke up and drove off. I didn't take my eyes off him during that time. After that I went to bed, reassured that Anne was all right. I'm just devastated about what's happened.'

'Did you see anyone else coming or going?'

'No.'

'No other cars draw up?'

'Nothing. Whoever killed her must have been very quiet.'

'Thank you for your time Madam.'

Back at the station she relayed this to Flare.

'OK', he said, 'assuming she's right and assuming Razor has no recollection of it, stoned out of his head as he probably was, we need more than this.'

'We do know she was killed somewhere between 1.15 and 2 am. The neighbour saw Anne coming back at one.'

'Razor's house has CCTV cameras all over it. Marylebone High Street is full of them. We may be able to position his whereabouts at the time of the killing.'

It didn't take Steele long.

'Razor's Gallardo was filmed speeding at 1.10 am in Marylebone High Street', she said. 'His home CCTV cameras had it stationed outside his house when Anne was killed, and there was clear footage of him entering the house at 1.15 am. The next time he left the house was when we arrested him.'

'Let him go', Flare said.

As they released him Razor said 'If you really think I killed Anne you shouldn't be running this investigation.'

McKleith looked at the sign that said Gloss Road and turned into the narrow street.

Uniform houses in a neat row.

An old woman was putting up some washing and he glared at her as he passed. She looked away. He walked to number 24 and stood at the gate. There was no one about.

He stood there for a while looking for signs of life before walking off.

51

Lucinda, drunk, phoned Jack, only to get his voicemail. Putting on her nicest voice she said 'Darling Jack, give me a ring.'

She sat holding her glass close to her while outside the day passed by. She was a lot drunker when she heard her mobile ringing.

'Hello? Jack, how are you? Good to hear it. Oh, you know, apart from the syphilis you've given me, can't complain. Yes. You bastard. Why didn't you tell me? You've got a lot of explaining to do.'

He hung up and she hurled her phone across the room.

Ben left on another business trip that morning and said goodbye to Gertrude with misgivings.

He saw her face at the window watching him drive away and wondered what he would return to and if she was even safe to leave around Maxwell and Mary. She'd never given him cause for concern as a mother before.

Alone, Gertrude looked around her perfectly spotless house. She put on her white gloves and ran her hand along the edge of the cupboards and the dado rails.

Not a speck of dust.

She removed them, thinking of how in peeling away a condom she would stare at the semen in it. Then she washed her hands.

She went upstairs and stood at the window staring down into the street below, her face a pale image retreating from the light in the polished glass. She breathed in the smell of detergent and ran her hand along her thighs. Then she found a small crack in the corner of the wall and began to peel away the paint. She removed layers of it and held the tiny fragments in her hand. Their whiteness reminded her of shaving foam and she went into the bathroom where she found an old tin of Ben's and emptied it into the basin. She dipped her hands into the thick smooth foam and heard the sound of a blade scraping the hard bristles on a jaw.

Jack Martins heard the bell ring and nervously opened the door to see Lucinda stand swaying in the hallway.

'Got anyone hiding in here?', she said.

'Look, I'm sorry Lucinda.'

She walked past him.

'I bet you are. Any women under the bed?'

'I don't screw around.'

'No, of course not.'

'I didn't even know I had it.'

'Stupid lie Jack.'

'It isn't a lie.'

'Now, why don't I believe you?'

'I haven't had an affair for ages until you.'

'How flattering, now aren't you going to offer me a drink?'

'It's not even twelve and you're already drunk.'

'You call this drunk?'

'Yes.'

'Oh, you should see me at night, Jack. This is what you've done to me.'

She walked into the kitchen and poured herself a glass of Sauvignon Blanc.

'I don't know who I caught it off.'

'Now, could it have been Martha Fornalski, or Samantha DeLonge, or one of the many other women you shag for sport, do you do it before you go to the golf club and brag about it? But you won't be doing that again will you, not after your little humiliation there.'

'Lucinda I'm telling you the truth.'

'I saw the letter!'

'What letter?'

'In your drawer. From the clinic. Saying you had syphilis. You knew and you still shagged me.'

'You snooped.'

'I was looking for something.'

'What?'

'You can't stand there and be morally outraged.'

'I'd only just found out.'

'You knew and you still went to bed with me. You've been passed around by every wealthy wife in our small select circle, we all enjoyed you and we knew we were sharing you. But be careful, you're a servant in our world and we can turn. We know what our husbands get up to, but we do not want them finding out about our affairs, we're meant to be watched.'

'I don't know what to say.'

'You bastard.'

She tipped her wine over him and walked towards the door.

'I'll pay for your treatment.'

'I don't need your money. In case you hadn't noticed, I'm married to a wealthy man. But be careful, Jack. If you can't keep it in your trousers just keep our indiscretion to yourself.'

Steele stayed behind after Flare left the station. She went into the office used by the crime scene examiners and opened Maurice Ray's drawers. She found a collection of disposable coloured contact lenses and an assortment of cameras. She realised she was breathing fast as she explored his world and she wanted to know more, she wanted to see him sexually aroused, and she resented the redundancy of her desire for him, feeling small and worthless. She found an address for him and made a note of it. When she left she felt hungry for release.

She found Mark standing on her doorstep when she got to her flat.

'You're avoiding me again', he said.

She opened the door and walked up the stairs carrying her shopping, aware of his footsteps behind her.

'I'm hungry', she said and began to cook.

They drank vodka and after eating she looked at him and wondered how far she could take it. She was pouring herself another glass when he reached behind her and cupped his hands over her breasts and she thought about Jack Martins and knew why she would never sleep with a man like him. She was out of his world. Anger and desire entered her and she unzipped Mark's jeans and leant and took him in her mouth, wanting to cuff him to the hot radiator.

He pulled her towards the bed, undoing her blouse and unhooking her bra. She pulled down his jeans and began masturbating him as he reached inside her panties and stuck his finger deep inside her.

'I know what you like', he said.

She was reaching for her cuffs when he grabbed them from her and threw her on the bed, shackling her to it before she could fight him off. She was struggling with him, but he held her legs and parted them, forcing himself inside her. He put a hand around her throat, squeezing hard and watching the veins stand out.

'Get the fuck off me', she said in a choked voice.

He pinched one of her nipples.

She could feel him pushing deep inside her and she looked at the ceiling, seeing a map of lines that seemed to lead her somewhere she didn't want to go.

As he came she kicked him, knocking him backwards.

Then she felt his hand tighten around her throat and squeeze. She was gasping for air when he released his grip. Mark inserted his finger inside her.

'Welcome to hypoxia', he said.

Steele wanted to fight as he rubbed her, but she was aroused and came quickly, pushing hard against his hand.

'You will find it addictive', Mark said.

He got dressed and uncuffed Steele. Then he left the flat.

She went into the shower. But she realised she didn't feel dirty.

52

The deals were falling into Brian Samson's lap and he needed a challenge. It was all too easy. Gertrude's number lay in his suitcase like a narcotic he was holding back for the evenings when his shadow wandered the streets in hungry exile from Mirabelle.

While he increased his profit margins one afternoon she was talking to Samantha DeLonge on the phone.

'I heard.'

'He was arrested in front of the golf club', Samantha said.

'What has he been up to?'

'Apart from screwing wealthy wives?'

'Well, he's never screwed me.'

'No, I know you don't go in for that sort of thing. I wouldn't look twice at him, but Lucinda has.'

'Really?'

'Apparently.'

'Does Max know?'

'I don't think so.'

'How did you find out?'

'Paul.'

'Well, then he'll tell Max.'

'Probably. I'm staying out of it.'

'And all for that creep', Mirabelle said.

'I know. She must have been desperate.'

'The police let Jack go.'

'Oh yes, I don't think he had anything to do with these murders.'

'There must be something in his past.'

'I wonder what.'

McKleith stared at the picture, its edges yellowed with time. The face was unfamiliar, a shape he tried to learn. He reached back into the past.

Then he got his coat and took the bus to the road. He walked down it seeing no one, sensing no one.

Jack Martins felt his isolation growing day by day.

He was ignored at the golf club and a lot of his calls went unreturned. He needed money, and without contacts he couldn't operate. He was leaving a tailor's in Mayfair when he heard someone call his name. He turned round to see Samantha standing there.

'Hello, Jack, long time no see.'

'Samantha, how are you?'

'Very well. Been shopping?'

'Yes. You?'

'I was meant to be meeting an old girlfriend for lunch but she just phoned to say she can't make it.'

'I don't suppose you'd join me?'

'For lunch? Why not?'

'Good.'

'It's not like you to be free for lunch Jack.'

'I'm glad I am.'

'Everything all right?'

'Well, you've probably heard I've had a few difficulties recently.'

'Oh?'

'Nothing that can't be resolved.'

'No, I haven't heard.'

'That's surprising.'

'You must tell me all about it.'

Gertrude put her plate down on the kitchen table.

She sliced the egg into thin sections and put the chopped celery on the side, cutting it into neat slices. Then she poured the tea from the pot. She began to eat, chewing slowly.

A noise from the front of the house roused her and she jumped from her chair and went to look out into the street.

A cat manoeuvered her wall. The street was empty. She sat down again and looked at her plate. Then she scraped the food into the bin.

53

Paul DeLonge was having lunch with Max Hereford.

They'd got through a few glasses of Chateau d'Yquem and Max noticed Paul kept looking at him as if he was weighing something up.

Paul had been on the verge of telling him about Lucinda and changed his mind, considering what it would do to their marriage. He poured himself another drink.

'Everything all right Paul?'

'Fine. How's business?'

'Very good. Just pulled off a massive deal worth two mill, Lucinda will be chuffed when I tell her, she wants a holiday home.'

'Somewhere hot?'

'Yes, she likes the country house, but she loves lying in the sun and Lucinda lying in the sun is a sight to behold.'

'Max.'

'Yes?'

'There's something I think you ought to know.'

'Oh?'

'I don't know how to tell you.'

'Well, just say it.'

'It's - difficult.'

'Oh come on, it can't be that bad!'

'It concerns Lucinda.'

'What?'

'She's been having an affair with Jack Martins.'

'Lucinda?'

'Yes. I heard from Samantha.'

'You must be wrong.'

'I don't think so. Speak to her, find out, I just thought you should be told.'

'I will speak to her. There must be some mistake.'

'Samantha seems pretty sure.'

'When did you hear this?'

'Only a few days ago. As you can imagine, I wasn't sure what to do.'

'You've done the right thing, even if you are wrong.'

'Here, let me settle lunch.'

That evening Steele went to the address she had for Maurice Ray. She sat in her car and looked for signs of him. His flat was dark and she was about to drive away when she saw him walk up the road with another man. They were both handsome in a way she liked. She watched them enter the flat and lights come on at the window. Then she drove away, a vein throbbing at her neck, the feeling of a hand gripping her throat.

THE PLEASURE OF
BEING WATCHED

54

Gertrude couldn't stop the dream entering her waking mind. It pierced the surface of her day like a shard of glass in her skin and she could hear a slow trickle of something within the house. She walked from room to room checking the taps. She stood outside inspecting the gutters. It wasn't raining and there were no leaks.

The face was like a permanent mark in her mind and she walked away from it. Each time she entered a room it followed her there. The lines hard as scars on dead skin.

He leaned over the kitchen sink, lathering his jaw, sharpening the open razor on the leather strop. Sometimes he would use it on her, grabbing her arm and lifting her skirt. The slap of the leather on her bare skin made her wince and she once bit through her lip so as not to cry out. She would stand in the hallway rubbing his finger marks from her numb arm. And he would shave, slowly, methodically, with sadistic satisfaction.

The face followed her to the supermarket and stared back at her from the shelves, and finally she sat exhausted in a chair.

Her house seemed unreal, her life, the distant husband, her children not her own.

The dream was always the same.

She stood at the end of a long garden with overgrown grass. Weeds climbed the rotting fence. The smell of something rank and rotten in the air, as if contagion was claiming nature.

Her mother crying from within, past the shuttered windows, past the open doorway where she stood clutching a toy.

Her father leaning over her mother, his red hand glistening in the single bulb's illumination that cast his shadow backwards towards Gertrude.

Her mother's face covered in blood, her eyes closed by bruising and her father turning.

She remembered his hand catching her elbow as she ran.

She remembered being dragged back into the house.

The social workers and endless parade of foster homes and the deep unhappiness more transit brought, the suffering at the hands of strangers, the endless humiliations and unspoken torture within her soul.

The shadows these happenings cast even death could not still, nor death's countenance within her own portrait of it.

The sudden sound of tearing flesh, the bleeding men on the bed she knew so well, punctured this still and dreaming recollection.

The clients' cries seeped like a lost threnody into the room. Her hand reached out for something and she wanted wounding more that food, more than air, she needed the precise point of contact with these men's expiation of their sins through death so that she may be its final arbiter and judge.

She reached for Gertrude Miller and found she had deserted her.

She feasted on the endless wounding like a disease eating itself.

55

As Lucinda got ready to go to Harley Street, Max returned from work.

He realised he wasn't going to catch her with Jack and that direct confrontation was the only way. The knowledge of the affair burned within him like an ulcer.

She was putting her make-up on as he climbed the stairs, their life together falling like a shadow within the house. He stood at the door unseen by her and thought how beautiful she was, how his property would be desired by other men. And in this watchfulness arousal merged with a desire to hurt her, as if some unknown part of him was growing in the spectacle she presented. He studied her movements to detect a difference from the way she was with him, as if he suspected their married life was part rehearsal on her part. Alone she may reveal something she hid from him. And he thought of all their friends, now diminishing as the killer removed them, and how their marriages interlocked in a web of lies.

The image of him in the mirror startled her.

'Max! What are you doing?'

She was standing in her bra and panties and she drew her arms about her to protect her nudity.

'What are you hiding?', he said.

'Nothing. You made me jump.'

'You don't want me to see you like that?'

'I thought you were at work. I thought there was an intruder in the house.'

She held her arms tightly across her chest and Max felt a surge of anger.

'You weren't expecting Jack?'

'Jack?'

'Yes.'

She let her arms fall and the image of her filled him with desire and a violent jealousy. He walked towards her.

'Max what is wrong?'

'Paul tells me you've been having an affair with Jack.'

'Paul?'

'Yes Paul.'

'He's crazy!'

He grabbed her arm.

'Tell me the truth!'

'Get off! You're hurting me.'

'Have you been having an affair with Jack?'

'Let go of me.'

He released his grip, and she stood there rubbing her arm, his fingerprints still embedded in her flesh.

'I have not been having an affair with Jack.'

'You've never slept with him?'

She sat on the bed. He looked at her, running his eyes down her body, desire and violence chasing each other in his brain.

'It was not an affair.'

'That's an admission.'

Her gaze was locked onto the carpet as she spoke.

'I slept with him. I'm so sorry, Max.'

'So it's true.'

'It only happened once.'

'How could you?'

She ran to the bathroom. He could hear retching noises as she stood over the toilet in the dark.

'It was a one-off.'

'You had an affair.'

'It wasn't like that.'

'What was it like?'

'A mistake. A mistake I regret more than you could ever know.'

'However you want to dress it up or play it down, it's your shame and guilt talking and your inability to look me in the face and tell me exactly what happened, how it happened, how much you desired that little playboy, what it felt like. If you could do that I'd have more respect for you now.'

'What do you expect when you play dangerous games Max?'

He took a step towards her.

'You know what we do, it's part of who we are.'

'Yes and you change your wives by doing it.'

'Why didn't you tell me?'

'I didn't tell you because I didn't want to hurt you.'

'No you didn't tell me because you wanted to keep your dirty little secret.'

'I'm sorry you found out this way.'

'But you're not sorry you did it.'

She stared at him with veiled eyes and he left the room.

As he slammed the door she finished getting ready and went to her appointment with Dr. Johnson.

Steele watched Maurice Ray walk past her in the corridor. He went into the men's changing rooms. There was no one around and she waited long enough for him to remove his protective clothing. Then she went in. She could hear the sound of water from the shower and she opened the door and stood there looking at him.

'What do you think you're doing?', he said.

'I want you Maurice.'

'I'm gay.'

'You're not.'

She reached out and touched him and slid her hand down to his penis.

'Do you like that?', she said.

'As you can see it does nothing to me.'

'Don't you want to touch me?'

'This is sexual assault.'

Steele backed off and left the changing rooms, returning to her office. As she walked away she caught a glimpse of a packet of More menthol cigarettes in his bag. All afternoon she could smell them, and feel Allen's hand on her mouth. She could see his eyes boring into her after he'd raped her, as if he was capturing the moment and her loss. And she thought of the killer she and Flare were trying to catch, and how he turned Anne Lacey's eyes to cameras.

56

Samantha DeLonge handed him the cash. She'd gone out in a track suit, trying to manufacture anonymity, and met him at the small grimy café. Now she wanted to turn her back on this man whose services she needed.

He counted it and said 'I'll get back to you when I've got the information.'

'I want to know if there is anything criminal in Jack's past.'

'I have contacts who can help me with that.'

'Anything else you find out I'll pay you for.'

She watched as he left the café and followed soon after.

Brian Samson left work that evening and drove to the flat.

Her unavailability certain nights of the week irritated him and he wondered about her other life. She existed for him on the edge of a contract. He rang and scaled the soiled stairs and waited for her to open the door. As she stood in the hallway light the lines around her eyes seemed harsh, unreal, as if she were someone else.

He looked over her shoulder at the flat.

'Go through', she said.

He undressed in the lurid light and as she watched him she wondered who these men were. They seemed like intruders in her home.

She went into the kitchen and fetched a bottle of Flash spray which she took through into the bedroom and began to squirt all over his penis.

He jumped up.

'What the fuck do you think you're doing?'

'You need cleaning.'

'I'm not into that, you've got the wrong client.'

He grabbed her arm.

'You're dirty and need cleaning', she said.

She began rubbing his penis, the foam dripping from him.

'Get your clothes off.'

He grabbed her gown, exposing her flesh, and she ran from him into the kitchen.

He followed her. She had her back to him as he walked up to her and she turned and he fell onto the kitchen knife. It stuck out of him rigidly and wobbled with the impact and he stood there trying to pull it out, shock and outrage sweeping across his face while Gertrude reached out and pushed it in further, stabbing him repeatedly until she was saturated with his blood and he staggered out into the hallway and lay on the carpet. She kept penetrating him like they did when they crawled on top of her, but this time she was doing it and she saw him covered in blood, head to foot, lying on the floor, more a ribbon than a man, some bleeding object falling away there and looking up at her as she felt his flesh fall apart beneath her hand, tearing and breaking with a soft sharp slicing noise. She was mesmerized by the sucking sound the knife made on withdrawal and the slow comfortable hiss of reentry, watching all he was fading from his eyes.

Gertrude felt his blood soak her dress, and she heard the chimes of an ice cream van at the end of a garden a long time ago.

She pulled the knife out of him and watched it drip back into his wound. The image of a man raping a woman, a calm statuette graven in her memory came alive now, his hips moving through the squalid air like a slow desecration of everything she'd ever considered holy, and she arched her neck as she stabbed him, his cries somehow female and an unmaking of him and all he was as a man, the rapid leeching of his fluids like some act of religious subversion.

When it was over she felt a tremor inside her like a trapped bird and she wondered where her heartbeat was.

She sat in the chair in the bedroom and tried to find the door to the garden.

Then she took all the knives and removed them from the flat, driving into the past through the black night.

57

Men don't understand female desire,
It is a strange vine interwoven with tendrils of hatred
The thorns born of anticipated rejection,
Narcissus's face broken in the pool.
To give them the mirror they seek is the key,
Belief in themselves and you.
They lacerate themselves on uncertainty and the man's job
is to abet that tide.
Think of them as a trace of belladonna in your rose bush.

The next day Gertrude went to a garden centre and bought some Astrantias. She took the knives from the boot of her car, dug two feet into the end of the garden and buried them, planting the Astrantias on top. She finished as Mary and Maxwell returned from school. She made them lamb kebabs for supper, lovingly placing the meat on the sharp skewers.

Jack waited for Samantha in the brasserie. He ordered a glass of Montrachet and sat drinking it slowly, unable to pay. He was angry and frustrated. Almost everyone had turned their backs on him and he felt this whole thing was being orchestrated by an unseen hand.

He resented the men whose wives he screwed, their money and their contacts, and knew he was an outsider. Samantha was his only shot. He would work her and get out, travel, start up somewhere else.

From where he sat he could see the street and watched for her. Some women walked by, a little common, dressed in the wrong clothes, laughing, a few of them drunk. They looked in his direction and he turned his back. Nothing there worth pursuing.

When Samantha walked in she looked stunning in a sleeveless satin Armani dress. She offered him a perfumed cheek and they ordered lunch.

'Like old times', she said.

'You and me?'

'Yes.'

She held her glass up.

'Samantha, you haven't aged a day.'

'You always know what to say.'

'You put most women in the shade.'

'Most?'

'All.'

Michael McKleith stood at the end of Gloss Road looking for signs of life. It seemed to him a deserted place where people hid from their pasts. And what he wanted lay there.

From time to time the silence was broken as a kid wheeled by on a bike. A neighbour came out with washing and hung it up, casting glances over her shoulder at him.

He smoked. He passed the house, stopping at the gate, peering through the lace curtains that hung in the window like a veil over agony.

He sought the face, unsure if he would recognise it. And he felt angry, as if something he owned had been stolen from him. He paced the area as if it was his private prison.

He returned to his hotel room and pored over the past like a map which held the coordinates of some buried loot.

PAYING TO BE KILLED

58

The undesired.
See them,
The women men do not want,
Who move with so much effort
Like ponderous cows.
No fuck luck with Mister Lust,
These brood mares
Hate the women men desire,
They pick the wrong clothes
They have no balance in their gait,
The reflection they see in the mirror is an invention,
A lie they tell themselves to carry on living.
But from time to time the image fails,
They see themselves in horror
And hide out in the job of children,
The excuse for their ugly wombs,
The repository of their sick psyches,
The wasteland of their undesirability.

When Ben returned from his business trip he found
Gertrude sitting alone in a darkened kitchen. Her hands

were knotted together and she was staring at the wall.

'What's wrong?', he said.

'A man has been following me.'

'What man?'

'I don't know, someone bad.'

'He followed you here?'

'Yes.'

'What does he look like?'

'I don't know, I don't want to know.'

'Gertrude, you're not making much sense. Have you called the police?'

'No.'

'Well, I will.'

'Don't!'

She went upstairs and he stood staring after her, feeling there was less and less of his wife and soon someone else entirely would be living there.

Suddenly the house felt invaded and unsafe. He poured himself a drink and gazed out of the window into the deserted street watching for figures hiding in the shadows. The only faces he saw were Maxwell's and Mary's as they returned from school.

59

At Jack's flat Samantha stretched and lazily got out of his bed. She padded about without any clothes until he wrapped a gown around her and handed her a glass of Besserat.

'You keep a good cellar', she said.

'Not for much longer.'

'Oh?'

'It's nothing. Just a few deals fallen through recently and the bloody banks, you know how it is.'

'No, I can't say I do. Paul has so much money.'

She looked at him then and saw his face change, some ripple of pain passed across it and left. She went over and put her hand on his chest.

'What's wrong?'

He dragged his hand through his blond hair and looked away.

'Come on, you can tell me', she said.

'I have a relative, a not particularly well relative I've been helping, I've given him too much and it's left me with nothing.'

'You're a good man.'

'I'm not a perfect man Samantha, not by any means.'

'Is it money?'

'I've got something in the pipeline, but I need a backer at the moment.'

She sipped her champagne.

'Mm, this is nice. Come back to bed.'

'And here I am boring you with my financial worries.'

She played with his zip.

'Maybe I can help you.'

'You?'

'Why not? Come back to bed.'

Before he called her a taxi she left him some cash. Enough to tide him over.

He saw her to the door and gave her a long lingering kiss that left her tasting desire all day, then he went back inside and looked in his bare cupboards.

His last bottle of champagne lay empty and he only had a few cheap bottles of wine left.

At home Mirabelle was growing desperate at Brian's absence. At first she thought he had another woman but dismissed the idea.

Now she was worried. She rang the police.

60

Razor got up, yawned, stretched, and went into the kitchen.

He decided on a few lines before leaving for the studio. After showering he checked his emails and walked into the garden for some air. He knew the whole thing with Anne would die down. He'd met another model. He tried her number, got her voicemail and left a message.

The sun hovered in the sky, it was going to be a hot day. He went back inside and closed the door. As he stood up he felt the most excruciating pain shoot through him.

He turned, but his muscles wouldn't work. Then another pain. He struggled and felt a hand restrain him. In the glass of the door he could see his reflection, cast there surreally, like some waking nightmare. He could feel the blood dripping from him and as he fell he reached for the face, seeing blackness.

Brian Samson's body lay in Gertrude's deserted flat.

His blood covered the hallway and the kitchen, seeping into the bedroom like some spectral guest. The smell was now so bad that when the postman delivered some junk mail, he caught a whiff of it through the letter box.

61

Max sat bleary eyed in his car outside Jack's flat.

He'd been there all night, drinking occasionally from the bottle of whisky by his side.

He'd expected to see Lucinda leave, but there had been no movement at all from the time he turned up. He thought of confronting Jack, of hitting him, and now just stared at the doorway that led to the person he blamed for the hurt he was feeling.

He switched on the ignition and drove home, where a startled Lucinda stood in the hallway as he entered.

'Where have you been?'

'Out', he said, marching past her upstairs.

She waited to speak to him but when he came down he was dressed and left for work.

Ben was in the bathroom when Gertrude made the offer.

'Would you like me to shave you?'

He caught her eye in the mirror and tried to think of an excuse, but before he could she started lathering his face.

He tried to pull away but she covered him in shaving cream and sat him in a chair.

'Dear dear', she said, 'all this bristle'.

The part of him that enjoyed the physical contact succumbed and he allowed her to proceed, scraping at his cheek and flicking the suds into the immaculate sink.

She leaned across him, her warmth palpable in the bathroom, and as she did, he noticed the plasters on her buttocks. He moved and she nicked his cheek.

'Hold still.'

His head raced and he wanted to stand up, but she held the razor close to his throat now.

The sound of scraping stopped as she pinched his nose and ran the blade down his upper lip.

When she was finished he rose and inspected himself.

'That's a close shave', he said.

'As a man should be.'

'Gertrude?'

'Yes?'

'Are you-?'

'What?'

He looked down at her legs, now covered again by her robe.

She followed his eyes.

'What?'

'Thanks.'

'It's a good razor.'

'Yes.'

The postman couldn't shake off the smell.

As he did his rounds, he kept thinking of it and when he returned the next day and caught another whiff of it, decided it was stronger. He called the police.

Max didn't go to work that day, but sat outside Jack's flat.

His head reeled with anger. He wanted a sighting of him, he wanted to feel how much he hated this man and to settle in his mind what he would do to him.

Finally at one o'clock he got it. A taxi drew up and Samantha got out. She rang the bell and disappeared inside. A few minutes later she emerged arm in arm with Jack and they walked straight past him.

62

She shops at Glamorous Amorous,
Nestling her soft cunt inside her Love Full Knickers,
Her flesh on display,
She craves the touch of Guia la Bruna.

The gardener found Razor's body.

His blood had sprayed from the back door to the wall in the next room, flecking the paintwork. It stuck to the lampshades and the pictures. He called the police and waited for them in the street.

Paul and Samantha were waiting for Max and Lucinda to arrive for dinner.

Max had been hurrying Lucinda along, but since things had got messy with Jack, she felt reluctant to see their friends. She felt Samantha was avoiding her. She left several messages which went unanswered. When they finally left they were late and he snapped at her in the car. She took it without saying anything.

At the restaurant Samantha greeted them warmly.

'Lucinda, lovely dress', she said, standing up.

They air kissed.

She offered her cheek to Max, who brushed her lips with his. A flicker in Samantha's eyes was soon brought under control.

'We were just about to order', Paul said.

The waiter hovered with bread.

'We have calves liver and game casserole as specials', he said.

'That'll do me', Paul said, snapping his menu shut. 'Wine?'

'I think I'll pass', Max said.

The waiter started taking their orders.

When he'd left, Lucinda turned to Samantha and said 'I hear you've been busy.'

'Oh?'

'Darling, I can't get hold of you for love or money.'

'Oh, you know how it is, with both love and money.'

She cast a sideways glance at Paul, who swigged his wine.

'Everything all right Max?', Samantha said.

'Fine, why shouldn't it be?'

As they ate the tension grew. Finally it was Paul's boasting that pushed Max.

'Just closed another big deal, I can't seem to stop making money.'

Max looked down at the food lying between them like an indigestible fact.

'I saw you leaving Jack Martins's flat today, Samantha.'

'What?'

'Looking like two lovers.'

Lucinda looked from him to her as Paul turned to Samantha.

'Is this bloody true?'

'I don't know what he's talking about.'

'That explains your good mood, you've been at it again.'

'Paul!'

'Go on admit it.'

She got up and walked from the table.

63

Flare and Steele stared at Razor's butchered body.

Maurice Ray looked at her behind his mask, then raised his Nikon D300 and began taking pictures.

'So he's linked to the same set as the others?', she said.

'The links are in the killer's mind', Flare said.

She looked at Razor's neck and noticed a hole on the side.

'He's removed something again', she said. 'First Anne then Razor.'

'He knows these people.'

Frank Norris told Flare and Steele that the killer had removed Razor's thyroid gland. Don Harvard turned up at the station just as they returned from the pathology lab.

'What are the body parts when you put them all together?', Steele said.

'Is there a pattern in them?', Flare said.

'Yes. If we take all these parts and put them together as a whole it might just tell us what he's doing with them.'

'If they represent power, the parts might show us what it is he thinks he's lacking.'

'He removed Larry Fornalski's Adam's apple and the thyroid gland is located under that', Harvard said. 'The parts he's choosing are not necessarily meaningful in the way you think.'

He could feel Flare's frustration.

'This isn't getting us anywhere', Flare said.

'We've got to work together if we stand a chance of catching this killer', Harvard said.

'So far your profile hasn't helped us find him.'

'All you've told us is his butchering of them would increase in its violence', Steele said.

Harvard nodded.

'What I mean Jackson, is that we need to put professional differences aside.'

'Professional differences?'

'I know your old school cop approach is in conflict what I'm doing here. I know you question my methods and are frustrated that we haven't caught him yet. And guess what? So am I. If you didn't believe I had anything to offer, you wouldn't have called me here.'

'How is Razor connected to the others?'

'That's what we need to find out. But the connection isn't solely going to lie in the social circles they kept, that's where you're getting this wrong.'

'How then?'

'What they represent to the killer.'

'A lifestyle he despises.'

'To him they're nothing more than organ bearers.'

'Yeah, well I say we check out doctors who've been struck off for malpractice in this area, anyone who performed dubious operations in the last ten years and who may have developed a psychosis around cutting out bits of people.'

'Maybe they're ex-clients of his', Steele said.

'Go ahead', Harvard said, 'look into it, it may lead you somewhere.'

'Have you got a better idea?', Flare said.

'All I know is this is not what it seems.'

When the police got to the flat and pushed open the letterbox the smell knocked them back into the street.

It lay above an electrical shop and there were no neighbours to ask about the comings and goings there. Since Gertrude conducted her business at night the shopkeeper had never seen her. The two officers forced the door and climbed the stairs into the mounting stench.

They kicked in the door to the flat. They saw dried blood on the faded carpet. Brian Samson's body had started to decay and flies settled in his rotting wounds, swarming at the officers as they entered the darkened hallway.

It wasn't long before they called Flare and Steele.

64

Paul DeLonge refused to speak to Samantha, moving from room to room while she followed him remonstrating about Max's disclosure.

'You don't really believe him, do you?', she said ,'he only said that to get back at you for telling him about Lucinda, I warned you.'

'You set it up! You wanted me to tell him so Jack could be all yours.'

'How ridiculous!'

'I know how you work.'

'There's no truth in it, why would I be interested in Jack Martins?'

'Because you're getting old and you're worried you're not as desirable as you used to be. He gives you your confidence back.'

She watched him walk away.

The butchery of Brian Samson threw Flare and Steele off any scent they thought they'd picked up of the killer.

The flat, the location, the fact that it looked like the room of a low-rent prostitute, all of it took them away from the ideas they'd started to form. Brian Samson looked like just another customer, and they wondered if in their investigation they'd been looking for the wrong gender of killer. He lay there hacked beyond human recognition.

'Could a woman have been doing this all along?', Steele said.

'She'd have to be strong.'

'It looks more frenzied this time.'

'If the killer's starting to lose control, then that's good for us.'

The body was naked and there were no clothes to be found. He had no ID on him. Meanwhile forensics dusted the flat.

65

As Ben left for work the images flooded Gertrude's mind.

She'd been unable to stop them coming in the night and lay awake next to her husband, who assumed the menacing form and face of a stranger in the pale twilight cast by the glow of the street lamp. Each time he turned over and touched her, she edged further away from him until she was almost out of the bed. Now as she watched him disappear at the end of the road she looked for the face she'd seen yesterday and pulled away from the window and the empty street.

She sat at the kitchen table with a cup of tea. It grew cold. The memories were taking hold. The beatings her mother took, the bruises covered by makeup. And then the time she tried to stop him.

She'd come in to find him standing over her mother, who lay on the kitchen floor with a swollen face. Gertrude pulled his arm away and he turned and struck her across the side of the head, knocking her against the wall. She had to miss school the next day.

She lived in dread of this man, who at the slightest provocation would launch into a tirade.

Friends tried to talk to him. He broke one of the

husbands' noses. His voice could switch to a certain nuance she knew and remembered all too well, a nuance that told of coming danger because he was displeased.

Forensics came back to Flare with something he wasn't expecting.

'More than one murder has been committed at the flat', he said to Steele.

'Could we be looking for a female serial killer who's started to kill her own clients?', she said.

'Forensics say there are blood stains on the walls and underneath the carpet, which has been newly and inexpertly laid.'

'How old?'

'Recent.'

'So her clients were visiting her in the room she was killing them in.'

'And paying for it.'

'And the body we found?'

'Brian Samson.'

'Who is he?'

'Wealthy banker, he's well placed in the Glamour Set.'

'This was a little down-market for him, don't you think?'

'There's no accounting for taste, these guys have some strange sexual proclivities.'

'Wealthy guy likes visiting the gutter.'

'We don't know anything about who rented the flat, we're chasing up the landlord.'

They went down to the pathology lab to see what Frank Norris had to say.

'This is a different style of killing', Norris said. 'The wounding is frenzied, whoever killed him was in a state of fear and stabbed him repeatedly.'

'Any organs removed?', Flare said.

'None.'

66

Michael McKleith counted out his remaining cash. He hadn't shaved since the job and his face was obscured by a thick growth of beard.

He cleaned his gun, slowly working his way through it piece by piece. The yellowed picture lay on the bedside table, a reminder of why he was there. Then he left the hotel.

Flare and Steele found out that Brian Samson had been married and paid a visit to a distressed Mirabelle, who sat nursing a cognac as they broke the news to her.

'Did he suffer?' she said.

Flare looked at the ground.

'He was killed in a brutal fashion, madam', Steele said, 'and we're trying hard to catch his killer, who we believe is a woman.'

'A woman?'

'Anything you think of, please let us know.'

Outside Flare turned to her and said 'You think she knows her husband visited prostitutes?'

'Are you going to ask her?'

Samantha met him in the same café.

She sat in the corner away from the window and watched him enter. He came over and set the manila envelope down on the tacky table in front of her. She opened it and peered inside at a page with Jack Martins's arrest details.

'Fraud?', she said.

'Apparently.'

'Now why doesn't that surprise me?'

'He was never charged, but then fraud is the hardest crime to bring to court.'

'Here's what I owe you', she said.

He counted it and stood up.

'Nice doing business with you.'

Steele stopped at The Fox on her way home. It was her local and was almost empty. She ordered a vodka and sat drinking it, unaware she'd been followed.

She went to the ladies. As she came out of the cubicle Vic Jones put his hand over her mouth and pushed her inside.

'A woman like you should get fucked in here', he said, reaching inside her trousers.

She was struggling but he had a strong grip and he began to undo her bra. She got her knee up and connected with his groin and pushed past him.

Vic was doubled over as she said 'If you do that again I'm going to make an official complaint.'

LIVING WITH GLASS

67

The street seemed old now, unlike the place she'd lived in and travelled down for years.

Gertrude walked to the shops, feeling the weight of the past on her.

She meandered through the desolate aisles, returning home, avoiding the faces she passed, afraid of seeing the one she dreaded, the one who would undo who she'd been.

Inside the house Ben's picture sat like a forgery. His face stared at her like a stranger's. She knitted her hands together, the fingers white, bloodless, as she crossed the carpet to the window. Its glass seemed too fragile, a form of insanity, and she wondered why people put up with it, living with glass. She ran her hand along its edge, checking the putty, ensuring it was intact. She calculated how easy it was to smash and retreated to the back of the room where she sat rocking.

His face came to her from the darkness.

Don Harvard was in the office with Flare and Steele.

'Brian Samson was killed by a prostitute, or a woman who's been doubling as a prostitute', Harvard said.

'We've got two killers', Flare said.

Harvard nodded.

'The killer you've been looking for all this time is not a prostitute.'

'Because no organs have been removed.'

'That is vital to the other killer's methods.'

'What if she just changed direction?', Steele said.

'No.'

'It's not the first time the killer's done that.'

'Whoever killed Brian Samson did not kill Larry Fornalski, Martin Gould and all the others. You have two killers', Harvard said.

'Why do you say she may be doubling as a prostitute?', Flare said.

'Because if she was just a prostitute, if she relied on it for her income, there would be some knowledge of who she was, she would have colleagues in the sex industry. The existence she led at the flat was covert and separate to her main life.'

'So what's her motive? Revenge?', Flare said.

'Who knows?'

'She just decides to start killing her clients, one of whom is wealthy and would fit as a victim of the other killer.'

'Psychosis happens all the time.'

'Do you think the two killers know each other?', Steele said.

'A collaboration? No.'

'But Brian Samson belongs in the other case.'

'Coincidence.'

'You think?'

Samantha arranged to meet Jack at his flat. As he greeted her with a warm kiss she noticed his case in the hallway.

'Going somewhere?'

'I thought I'd take a short holiday.'

'You're not running out on me are you?'

'No.'

'Good. Because I want you right here where I can enjoy you.'

She stroked his chest.

'Samantha you're married.'

'To Paul.'

'What I mean is, we don't have any claims on each other.'

'Oh but I do.'

He pulled away.

'I'm discreet and no one will ever find out about us but you can't make claims on me.'

'Is that a threat?'

'You've been great and I appreciate the money.'

'Jack, I have a little piece of paper in my pocket.'

'What?'

'That says how you were arrested for fraud.'

'Are you blackmailing me?'

'I'm just saying right now, I'm a friend. No one wants to know you. I enjoy your company, you enjoy mine. You don't want this getting out, then keep me sweet.

If you play your cards right I can help you get back into those circles that are presently shut for you.'

68

He sat in front of the altar.

The incense in the church was overpowering and sent him into a reverie which summoned the images.

Beyond his field of vision a priest walked across the church.

Christ lowered down at him. He saw filth in the pews, excrement gathering in a black tide and washing through the aisles, carrying with it the unspeakable sins of the penitents.

Behind the confessional box lay abominable acts, beneath the cassock lies. He caught his breath at the general decay of mankind.

Jack Martins opened the front door of his flat and peered down the road. He looked different, less urbane, as if the stress was changing his looks. He locked the front door and walked quickly away from his flat. There was anger in his steps as he disappeared at the end of the road.

69

Gertrude wrapped the towel around her hand to stem the blood. The shard of china lay in the sink, a swirl of pink fading from its edge as she ran the tap on it.

Upstairs in the bathroom cupboard she pushed the tampons aside in anger and sought out the plasters, sticking one over the cut and rinsing her fingers. She fled from herself into the bedroom where she lay with her back to the mirror, seeking refuge from the knowledge of who she was. She smelt Ben on the pillow next to her and got up, seeing dust in the corner, wondering where it had blown in from.

In the hallway the fractured vista into her children's bedrooms brought the smell of the flat into the house, some distant place she'd known long ago which reeked of body fluids and the wash of men's filth. A bead of sweat crawled down her legs like an insect and she scratched herself, digging her nails deep into her skin until it bled and she gained momentary release.

She felt hot and went downstairs. As she reached into the cleaning cupboard her mother's face came to her. It was covered in pain and she was asking something from her which she knew she didn't have, leaving her feeling empty and alone.

Perhaps it was this aloneness that led her to the door before the bell rang. The noise startled her. Thinking it was the postman she opened it.

In the sudden avoidance of the stark realisation the opening brought she tried to draw the postman's face upon his, fleeing from the knowledge of him and all he represented. The lines she sketched with a lifetime's denial faded there as did her married life. She looked into the reality of his presence there on her doorstep, her eyes fixed on the filthy beard that did little to disguise him to her. She could smell tobacco in the bristle.

'Hello Gertrude', he said. 'Aren't you going to invite your father in?'

He walked past her into the living room where he looked at the pictures.

Gertrude followed him in and Michael McKleith sat looking at her.

'What do you want?', she said.

'To see my daughter.'

'After all these years.'

'Yes.'

His voice was like an echo, and the room seemed enormous suddenly, the walls moving a little as she sat down and tried to steady herself, reaching for something she knew, a gesture or a word on which she could prop herself until he was gone.

'How did you find me?'

'It wasn't hard.'

'Why?'

'Why what?'

'Find me. Here.'

'It's been a long time.'

'I don't remember you.'

'You knew my face just now all right.'

'You've haunted me. Those things you did.'

'All a long time ago Gertrude.'

'Dreadful things.'

'Life moves on. Mind if I smoke?'

'You killed her.'

He lit a cigarette and took a deep drag and blew it up towards the ceiling. Then he turned and looked her full in the face.

'You've been looked after and I've been away. I've done my time for what I did and it was all a long time ago.'

'It was yesterday.'

'Remember the garden?'

He stood now and she watched as he held the burning end of his cigarette to his lips.

She knew what he wanted.

'Tea?'

'Yeah, wouldn't mind.'

She walked past him and opened the window. An ice cream van passed down the street and she was back. The garden surrounded her with its lost promise of protection, her refuge from the pain violated by this man who was sitting in her living room. As the noise tinkled in the afternoon air she saw it. He was standing with his razor in his hand and her mother's blood dripped onto the grass. Beyond his shoulder she could see her mother's legs by the open door to the house she didn't want to enter. She ran from him to the end of the garden and pulled on the door that led outside, but it was overgrown with ivy. He was gaining on her and his shadow covered the door, and she ran towards the house and the room with her mother in it that she didn't want to enter. He was threatening her. Suddenly the chimes stopped and she heard sirens.

As Gertrude turned from the window he reached for her hand and she pulled away, tensing her neck and back.

'Don't take on Gertrude, I'm your father.'

'What do you want?'

'To see you.'

'What do you really want?'

'I told you.'

She left him and went into the kitchen and put the kettle on.

When she returned he was holding Ben's picture.

'Put that down.'

'Been married long?'

'I don't know.'

'What kind of an answer is that Gertrude?'

Every time he said her name she felt defiled, as if a wandering client had strayed from the flat into her house.

'I'll get the tea.'

She made two cups and brought them through and sat watching him while he drank, recalling the crude gestures and actions of the man she knew all those years ago in another life that hovered now at the edge of her existence like a venomous insect that had blown in on a foreign wind.

'I could do with some money', he said.

'And you'll go away?'

'I didn't say that.'

'Do you think I wanted to grow up in those homes?'

'It can't have been as bad as all that. You seem to have done all right.'

'Do you know what they did to me?'

'Nice tea.'

'After what you did?'

'You've got two kids. Nice.'

He held their picture up.

'You'll never meet them.'

'Who said I wanted to?'

'You just thought you'd turn up here and see me?

'Yes.'

She looked at him, the dull eyes, the hard face, and she saw his hands move across the edge of the cup, knowing in that instant that with them he'd moulded her life, formed her into the suffering she'd undergone while trying to live, and now he'd come back for payment. Inside her clenched fist the plaster turned red.

She turned her hand and looked at it, a taste like metal forming in her mouth, and she knew where the years had been leading him as he traversed the quiet misery of the road that took him there.

'Do you really know what you're looking for?', she said.

'You.'

'You don't even know me.'

'You're my daughter.'

'That doesn't mean anything, not when you've done what you did.'

'I've been punished.'

'Punished! You don't know the meaning of the word.'

He watched as she walked into the hallway and stood looking out into the street.

He could hear her go upstairs.

When she returned she walked over to where he stood.

He turned round just as she knew it, knew it all as she felt herself being fucked by strangers, the sweat on the men dripping onto her and the cleaning rising like a shower out of the darkness, the smell of bleach deep in her nostrils, masking another smell that lay embedded there and she felt the Cut Throat razor and saw his flesh tearing beneath the cheap suit he wore shiny already from sitting on buses and saw the red stain stretch its way across his neck and she pushed and pushed again digging deeper into the wound feeling now the meaning of the penetration she was subjected to the power and the yielding all in a rush as he screamed and she was in the flat again away from this life and he lay without moving, something she would need to tidy up.

70

Ben arrived at work to find he'd left some urgent files at home.

The time of his meeting precluded the use of public transport, so he got in a taxi and headed back. He felt tired and was worried about Gertrude. Seeing his street swing into view he leant forward.

'This is it, Gloss Road.'

He didn't expect to find Gertrude at home. It was the smell that stopped him in the hallway. Like someone had opened a foul smelling can that had polluted the air.

There in the living room lay a body so hacked and torn it didn't seem human. A swollen gash in its chest looked like lips on a diseased mouth.

Ben saw his wife moving in the kitchen, setting her cleaning fluids on the table.

As he moved forward she saw his face, registered the enquiry and shock written into it and said 'He wouldn't leave me alone.'

'What have you done?'

'All those years, Ben, he wouldn't let me be, and coming here, like that.'

'Who is he?'

'The man who has stood between us all this time.'

'Who?'

'Ben I will deal with this.'

'Do you think you can wash this away?'

'What else is there to do now that it's over?'

'Did he attack you?'

'Yes.'

'Are you hurt?'

'Oh, you have no idea what it's been like.'

'Where did he hurt you?'

'Here.'

She pointed at her head.

'No.'

'It's what he did to my mother.'

'Your mother?'

'Yes.'

'Is he the man you say has been following you?'

'All those years and coming here like that.'

'What did he do to your mother?'

'He beat us, both, her most of all, I was little you see and would hide in the garden, but he caught me once and gave me such a thrashing, men like that are all bullies, you've never hit me Ben, you're a good husband I don't deserve you, but he wouldn't go away, not now and not in my head where it hurts most. He was the reason I went to those foster homes, and all the things that happened there, he is the reason for all of this, Ben.'

He stared at her down a long tunnel and she suddenly came into focus.

71

He laid the jars in a neat row.

The light caught the glass, illuminating the flesh inside them. He gazed at them, poring over their contents. Beneath the still and silent crucifix he considered the flesh, its arcane and ritual significance, its slowness to decay, the preservation he could keep it under, and he wondered where the animation went when the light was darkened.

Jack was less than pleased with Samantha's assumption she could buy him. He was used to playing the field and she was not going to tie him down.

He looked around at his flat and weighed the situation up. Starting somewhere else would prove time consuming and if she could get him back into the old circle then he could make some money, enough to serve his purposes.

He resented the people he regarded as friends turning their backs on him and knew a thing or two about their private lives, especially what had been passed onto him in the form of pillow talk. Once he was back in, this would prove useful.

As he was about to go out, he heard the buzzer. He waited as Samantha made her way up.

'You look stunning', he said.

'Don't I always?'

'Of course.'

'Lunch?'

'Sounds good.'

'Then I fancy a spot of shopping, and thought you could tag along.'

He hid his irritation.

'I've got some appointments.'

'Nothing you can't cancel Jack.'

'Well actually.'

'Come on I'm paying.'

She grabbed his arm and headed out into the street with him.

Ben managed to get to the phone while Gertrude busied herself cleaning.

He steadied his hands and picked the receiver up. His wife's strange behaviour and his concerns about her mental health flashed through his mind and led him to the dead body in the other room. As he dialled emergency services he wondered if there was anything he could have done.

'Police please.'

He went outside and paid the taxi driver and returned to the hallway where he waited.

Gertrude was unaware of him and anything outside

what she was doing, and he watched as she scoured the kitchen work surfaces. He tried to figure out how long she'd existed in another world.

72

Paul DeLonge had taken to drinking at the office during the day and plotting his revenge. He was tired of upstarts like Jack Martins.

He flicked on the FTSE to check the latest share movements. He wanted to make a lot of money today.

After a while he went over to the bar and poured himself a cognac. He sat letting it warm him and saw Jack Martins's face. He knew people who could hurt him.

He would make sure Martins never went near his wife again. He looked at her picture and rage swept over him. He picked up the phone and cancelled her credit cards.

As he thought of Martins's address an idea came to him. He was sure a friend of his owned the lease on the property.

A quick call confirmed it. He would call in a favour. Martins would no more be part of the Mayfair set.

When the police arrived at Ben Miller's house they found him standing in the hallway keeping watch over Gertrude who greeted them from the kitchen.

'Tea, officers?', she said, and continued with her housework.

They went through into the living room and looked at the body. Ben stood in the doorway.

'Do you know who he is?', one of the officers said.

'I think he's my wife's father.'

The two policemen exchanged glances, disbelief working its way across their faces as they tried to register the implications of the crime.

'Did you witness it Sir?'

'No. I was coming back for something and found him here.'

'But your wife told you she did this?'

'Not in so many words.'

One of them radioed for back up.

'We need to talk to her Sir. What exactly did she say to you?'

'She's not making a lot of sense.'

'You knew the gentleman?'

'No.'

'So you came in and found him like this Sir?', the officer said.

'Yes.'

'And where was your wife?'

'In the kitchen cleaning.'

'Cleaning?'

'Yes.'

'Did you touch the body when you came in?'

'No.'

'I'll have to ask you stand outside Sir.'

He went into the hallway.

After a while the officer said 'I need to talk to your wife.'

He went into the kitchen and closed the door.

When he came out he said to Ben, 'Does she know what she's done?'

'I don't think so.'

'But she admitted it to you.'

'She's not well.'

'Does she suffer from a mental condition?'

'I think she does.'

'We're going to have to interview both of you.'

'Of course.'

He looked at the pictures in the hallway.

'I can see you have kids, you better make arrangements to have them collected from school.'

73

Max and Lucinda had been arguing regularly since the revelation of her affair with Jack.

Despite her best efforts she couldn't get close enough to reassure him it was a one off and she regretted it.

She spent her days getting drunk and thinking how to get even with Samantha. The fact that Samantha was about to get a nasty surprise was one thing that gave her pleasure.

Jack didn't care and was probably infecting every woman he came across.

That morning Lucinda walked about her house with a wine glass in her hand. She hadn't bothered getting dressed and was still wearing her nightie.

As she took a deep swig of Chardonnay she felt herself being pulled backwards. Something lanced her breast and she saw a red patch forming on the silk. She struggled, dropping the glass.

She tried to see his face. As he bent, the lights caught the crystals of his mask and Lucinda thought of all the thousand bright designer brands that filled her world.

Then she felt herself being torn, her flesh was being

cut to pieces. She felt a warmth running over her and a hand reaching inside her and moving there as she drifted in and out of consciousness.

She tried to steady herself, but her hand slipped in her own blood.

In moments she heard his voice, distant and familiar as an echo.

'You liked to know your nudity aroused men didn't you?', he said. 'You liked your Aubade, Sensuality, Complicity, Creativity and Glamour. You showed off that little ass of yours, wrapped neatly in your panties. You Boite A Desir. Were you the forbidden lesson? Absolument Glamour is why you wore it, and now I see all of you.'

He stripped the nightie from her and took from his bag a sackcloth which he laid over her naked and bleeding body. Then he cut an angular A into her neck.

The police who arrested Gertrude soon realised that there was something to the case that lay beyond a regular domestic scene that had ended in murder.

Gertrude's thin grip on sanity was evident to them as was Ben's incomprehension at what had happened. One of the officers knew about the recent murder of Brian Samson. He put a call through to Flare.

74

'Do we know who the victim was?', Flare said.

The officer who'd conducted the interview with Gertrude had put in some background checks.

'Michael McKleith, Gertrude Miller's father.'

'Her father?'

'That's right. Apparently, she hadn't seen him since her childhood. He'd just got out of prison.'

'What was he in for?'

'Murder. His wife.'

'The perp's mother?'

'Yes.'

'So he gets out of prison and tracks Gertrude Miller down and she kills him', Steele said.

'That seems to be it. We've pieced together bits from background checks and what she's saying but she's not making a whole lot of sense.'

'Do you think she's hiding something?', Steele said.

'I think she's mentally ill.'

'What about the husband?', Flare said.

'He doesn't know a lot. Never met the father.'

'I think we'll speak to him first.'

'He says his wife's been behaving in a very

disturbed fashion for some time, suspects she may have been leading a double life.'

'Doing what?'

'He's not sure. He says she cleans all the time and switches between two characters, one he doesn't recognise.'

'Does she work?'

'No.'

'Is he aware that she goes out for long periods of time that she can't account for?'

'He hasn't mentioned it.'

'Does she have a history of violence?'

'There's nothing on record. Her husband says she grew up in foster homes after the death of her mother, never saw the father again and never mentioned him.'

'We'll speak to the husband.'

The officer went to get Ben.

'You think this could be our other killer?', Flare said to Steele.

'You mean she doubles as a hooker and starts killing her clients?'

'Something like that. If it is her then at least we've got one case solved.'

'And Brian Samson? He was never part of her world.'

'Just stumbled into it.'

75

Ben Miller sat rigidly staring ahead at the wall as they walked in. A cup of coffee was going cold in front of him.

'Mr. Miller, I'm Chief Inspector Flare and this is Inspector Steele.'

'I can't believe any of this', he said.

'I understand you must be in shock Sir.'

'That Gertrude did this.'

'You say you came in and found your wife in the kitchen.'

'Yes.'

'And where was Mr. McKleith?'

'In the living room.'

'And he was dead?'

'He couldn't have been alive, not in that state.'

'Could you describe the state you found your wife in?'

'She was acting normal.'

'Normal?'

'As if nothing had happened.'

'Has she ever done anything like this before?'

'Killed someone?'

'Displayed violent tendencies.'

'No.'

'You say you've been worried about her mental state.'

'Yes.'

'Could you tell us a bit more about that?'

'She's been acting strangely for weeks.'

Flare could see he was struggling and waited for a few moments.

'How has her behaviour been strange?', Steele said.

'She's been distant, saying odd things.'

He took a sip of coffee and set the cup down.

'She was cleaning when you came home.'

'Yes.'

'And the body was in the other room.'

'Gertrude has this thing about cleaning, it's obsessive, she can't seem to stop it.'

They interviewed Gertrude next.

She sat making eye contact with Steele, avoiding Flare, but there was something opaque about her eyes when Steele looked into them. Flare noticed every time he asked her a question she looked at Steele, so he let her take over the interview.

'Mrs. Miller, could you tell us what happened?', Steele said.

'He came back.'

'Who came back?'

'The bad man.'

'Your father?'

'He hit mummy. I used to hide.'

'Your father used to hit your mother?'

'I tried to stop him once and he did it, it hurt.'

'And did he come to your house?'

'He was always there.'

'In your house?'

Gertrude began to rock on her chair. Her face opened and Steele realised she was interviewing a child.

'He said it was because mummy didn't clean well, so I did it.'

'Clean?'

'Mm. But it wasn't, he was just making excuses.'

'What excuses?'

'To hit her.'

'And then he did something very bad didn't he?'

'Mm.'

'Something he was sent away for.'

'They sent me away.'

'Your father went to prison didn't he?'

'He hurt mummy.'

'You never saw him again.'

'Daddy was bad and the homes were bad.'

'The foster homes?'

'They did things to me.'

'Gertrude?'

'Horrible horrible men. You're one!', she said looking at Flare.

He shifted uncomfortably in his chair.

'What happened when your father turned up at your house?', Steele said.

'They were all like that.'

'Was he following you?'

'Yes. And the others. They all followed me, that's why I took them there, I didn't want Ben to see it.'

'See what?'

'The blood.'

Flare and Steele exchanged glances.

'Who are the others?', Steele said.

'There was the first one. He stood outside my window. I gave him what he wanted.'

'What did he want?'

'Oh it's filthy isn't it, you understand what I'm talking about.'

'Where did you take them Gertrude?'

'Into the other room.'

'What happened there?'

'Sex! That's all they want! Then you have to clean up.'

'Is that what you were doing when the police arrived?'

'There's always so much to do.'

'Did you kill your father?'

'They would lie there wanting it and of course there was no other way to stop him coming back, so I got rid of them.'

'How did you get rid of them?'

'It only made the cleaning worse of course, they made such a mess. If it wasn't their dirty habits making a mess everywhere it was their blood.'

'Can you remember what happened when you opened the door and saw your father standing there?'

'The last one lay there saying filthy things and I cut him.'

Flare looked at Steele.

'Where were you when you cut him?'

'In the room.'

'At your house?'

'No. Never there, it never happened there.'

'So where was this other place?'

'They liked coming to my flat. Wealthy men with nothing better to do. I saw one of them on TV. Fornalski, that was the name. Someone killed him. I didn't. Some other woman killed him. They would lie there with their things hanging out wanting me to do it, like the other ones before.'

'Your father?'

'He stood there wanting money. Money I'd made to get rid of him.'

'And how did you get rid of him?'

She looked Steele right in the eyes. The little girl was gone, there was someone else sitting there.

'You clean them away.'

'How did you use money to get rid of him?

'They paid me and he went away.'

'Except he came back.'

'He wouldn't stop following me.'

'And he came to your house.'

'Yes.'

'And what happened?'

'I had to stop him.'

'And how did you do that?'

'The way I stopped the others. There was the one in the white coat who followed me.'

Flare and Steele exchanged glances.

'Did you hurt him Gertrude?', Steele said.

'Do you know what they wanted to do to me?'

'Were they trying to have sex with you?'

'That's what they call it.'

'And you defended yourself.'

'Yes! Mummy couldn't.'

'You stopped them.'

'They wouldn't listen.'

'Where did you do it Gertrude?'

'At the flat. He followed me.'

'Where did he follow you?'

'To the garden, I hid there.'

'The garden at your house?'

'The knives are under the Astrantias. There were always Astrantias growing at the end of the garden.'

'This was at your home.'

'It was safe at home.'

'Until your father turned up.'

'He hadn't shaved. Don't you see I had to stop him.'

Outside Flare turned to Steele.

'It's her', he said.

'Yes.'

'So she sees clients at a flat where she tries to keep her demons at bay until they come bursting out and she starts killing the punters.'

'Running from her father's shadow all these years.'

'She also killed Harlan White. The flat she used to see her clients was near the address I found for White. Don's theory pans out. She's not a prostitute in the real sense of the word, she's someone who was using it to stem the tide of her insanity. And that's the problem.'

'What?'

'She's certifiably insane.'

'So what do we do?'

'We get the psychiatrists in, they'll section her and she'll be sent away for a very long time.'

'At least the kids have another parent.'

'This is a tragic case.'

'Which leaves us with another killer out there.'

'Who is a whole different kettle of fish.'

WIVES' DESIRES

76

Max was drunk when he returned home and stumbled on Lucinda's body in the hallway. He stared in amazement at the desecration of his wife, as if this too were some final act of betrayal on her part, looking like a wasted beggar beneath the sackcloth, then he rushed to the telephone.

When the police arrived he was half way through a bottle of malt and slurring his speech.

It wasn't long before Flare and Steele got the call.

Three psychiatrists interviewed Gertrude Miller. They asked her the routine questions for determining the extent of her dissociation from reality. They noted that she continued to refer to her past as if it belonged to someone else. The sexual content of her dialogue became more graphic during the interview.

Afterwards they discussed her case and the most senior among them gave Flare and Steele the upshot.

'She has a dissociative personality disorder caused by a background of extreme childhood abuse.'

'So she's not fit to stand trial.'

'No. We'll be sectioning her.'

77

Lucinda Hereford's murder reminded them the other case was still very much alive.

'This time he removed her womb', Frank Norris said.

Steele looked at him in disbelief.

'He cut her womb out and walked away with it?'

'That's right.'

'To do what?'

Frank Norris shrugged beneath his mask, his eyes indifferent and clinical.

When Don Harvard came in Steele asked him the same question.

'Not so much to do what, but to make what', Harvard said.

'Do we have another killer on our hands who won't stand trial?', Steele said.

'Don't confuse it with the other case. Gertrude Miller was operating from a deep seated sense of sexual damage and abuse and her rage was directed against male sexuality. This killer is very different and is not insane.'

'He just removes women's wombs and takes them away for fun', Steele said.

'I'm not saying he's mentally well, I'm saying he's not insane.'

'What's the difference?'

'Gertrude Miller only half knew what she was doing. This killer knows exactly what he's doing.'

'So what's he building?', Flare said.

'Himself.'

'What?'

'He's empowering himself with their body parts.'

Paul DeLonge put the phone down and opened a bottle of Morey-Blanc. It was cold and smooth and biscuity. Below him the skyline of London stretched out like an inviting mistress.

Jack Martins would soon find it difficult to stay at his flat. Paul sipped from his glass, feeling that life was good again. There was only the small matter of Samantha to deal with. She had to be taught a lesson. She was an important part of his empire and he couldn't have her straying. More importantly, he didn't want word getting out about her affair with the low life who would soon have no life.

He thought about what had happened to Lucinda. His world was under threat. He had to keep it where he wanted it. He just needed to hit Samantha where it hurt her most.

78

Samantha hadn't been feeling well ever since she heard the news about Lucinda's murder. At first she thought it was the shock, the shadow of the killer falling against her window pane. He seemed to hover at the edge of their existence, an unglamorous intruder in a glamorous world. Then she realised her symptoms were physical.

Eventually she made an appointment to see her doctor and was angry when he suggested she had venereal disease. Once she'd expressed her outrage and shock, she said 'My husband must have been up to something', and walked out of the surgery.

The immediate explanation seemed obvious.

She made an appointment to go to a private clinic and waited until then, thinking what she would do to Jack if he'd given something to her.

The idea that disease was being passed around her exclusive set angered her.

At the clinic she sat with her fury building inside her. The doctor examined her and took a blood test.

During the time she waited for the results she only saw Jack once. They made love and afterwards she said to him 'There's nothing you're not telling me is there?'

'Like what?'

'Something I should know now that we're sleeping together.'

'I'm not seeing anyone else, if that's what you mean.'

'No, that's not what I mean.'

'Then what?'

'You know Jack Martins you're a mystery, you make love to me so gently sometimes, at others you are a little too rough in bed. Are you angry about something?'

'I'm not angry about anything. I can modify my lovemaking to suit you Samantha.'

He raised himself up on his elbow and looked at her and she drifted into his eyes.

'Is there anything you think I should know?', she said.

'Samantha, you're not making a lot of sense.'

He got up and walked into the bathroom and she followed, leaning on the door, watching him. He turned on the tap and bent and splashed water on his face in a gesture at once timeless and erotic, made more so by his being watched by her and she remembered falling the first time she saw him, as if he'd opened a trapdoor. She looked at his tanned and muscled arms as he bent and slipped on a pair of trousers, the muscles so accentuated she craved more of him.

She started getting dressed.

'You know Guia la Bruna suits you. That Love Bow Bralet is perfect for your breasts', he said.

'Glamorous Amorous is full of sexy things', she said.

She left his flat and took a taxi to go shopping.

When the test results came through the doctor said matter of factly 'You have contracted syphilis.'

'What?'

'It's treatable, but you need to tell your sexual partner.'

'I will.'

He wrote her prescription. That evening she went to see Jack. As he was pouring her a glass of wine, she threw the prescription in his face.

'I want an explanation.'

He stared at her and picked it up.

'I don't understand.'

'No nor do I.'

'What is this?'

'A prescription to treat the syphilis you've given me.'

Despite his best efforts she caught the flicker in his eye.

'Samantha I didn't know.'

'Oh don't give me that. You didn't care, thought you'd use me and give me a little something extra.'

'I only just found out myself, I was going to tell you.'

'Oh what, Lucinda gave it to you, did she?'

'She must have.'

79

Paul's mood was irritating Samantha.

She was angry with Jack and the more cheerful Paul became the more it aggravated her.

Finally she said 'What are you so happy about?'

'Why shouldn't I be?'

'Work?'

'What about it?'

'Normally, when you've just made a fortune, you're like this.'

'No, nothing to do with it.'

'What then? Have you forgotten one of our friends has just been killed?'

'Do I need a reason to be happy? I'm married to a beautiful wife. Later we can go upstairs and make love. Everything all right?'

'I'm not feeling very well.'

'Oh dear.'

'I think I'll go and lie down.'

'I'll be up later.'

When he entered their darkened bedroom Samantha was asleep.

He rose early the next morning and left for work before she was up. Her mood hadn't improved and she decided to treat herself to some retail therapy. She picked out some new handbags and at the till found that all her cards were refused.

'The organs, the body parts may not make sense in themselves', Harvard said, 'but they are to him an empowerment of who is he, who he may have once believed himself to be. He's reinforcing himself.'

'Reminds me of Frankenstein', Flare said.

'Victor Frankenstein made a monster which from a psychoanalytical perspective represented his shadow, that part of ourselves we don't like, which we reject and conveniently project out there onto other people, usually the people we clash with.'

'This guy's already a monster, of course he's running from himself.'

'Are you saying that he needs this mutilation to stem his trauma?', Steele said.

'More than that. He takes parts of his victims away to fill the abyss, the abyss he's in when he kills them.'

'So he goes on cutting people up, eventually the habit will stop working.'

'Exactly, that's when he'll need to do something more.'

'So what do the parts tell us about his psyche?', Flare said.

'Inside he feels he's missing something vital that makes other people tick. He needs to take his victims' body parts away and use them to give him what he's missing, what he feels has been missing from him all these years, maybe all his lifetime.'

'Is this guy holding down a job?'

'Hard to tell. Maybe, because if he's truly split, he'll be killing from an entirely different part of his personality.'

80

Steele met Mark at her flat that evening. She kept thinking of the last time and how she felt. The sensation wouldn't leave her. The orgasm she'd experienced was heightened, stronger than any she could recall.

'The way it works', Mark said, as he undid her blouse, opening each button slowly, 'is to do with neurochemistry. The neurotransmitters can make you hallucinate, did you experience that as you came Mandy?'

'No.'

She watched as he pulled her breasts over the top of her bra and started to rub her nipples.

'You felt high when you came.'

'Yes.'

She wanted to push him onto the bed and take charge but the need to feel it again was too strong and so she let him guide her.

'You don't need expensive lingerie, you are going to have the best orgasm of your life.'

He unzipped her skirt and lowered it, touching her through her panties.

'Wet.'

'Yes.'

Mark placed one hand around her neck, squeezing slightly.

'The carotid arteries carry blood full of oxygen to the brain. When I squeeze, you get carbon dioxide. That makes you feel high.'

He pulled down her panties and placed a finger inside her.

'All of this heightens the sensation when I touch you.'

Steele undid his belt, opened his trousers, and pulled out his penis.

'Come over to the bed.'

As she lay down Mark tightened his grip around her neck, watching the veins throb.

'It's as strong as cocaine', he said, as he placed his other hand between her legs and rubbed her.

Steele saw shadows, masked faces enter the room and she began to gasp. Mark increased his rhythm and she pushed against his hand. She saw Jack Martins. He was naked and on top of her, saying, 'Mandy I am going to fuck you and kill you. I fuck all the wives before I kill them.' She seemed apart from her body and could hear her gasps increase in frequency. Then the orgasm flooded her. She lay there while Mark removed his hand and looked at her.

'I know what you like Mandy', he said.

When Paul got home from work that evening, he found Samantha standing in the kitchen with a glass of wine in her hand.

'Hello darling', she said.

A saucepan bubbled behind her.

'Cooking dinner?'

'Yes. I thought I'd surprise you.'

'What is it?'

He sniffed the air.

'You want to know?' She lifted the lid, letting some steam escape into the room. 'Your ties.'

'What?' He went over to inspect the contents. Inside his ties lay boiling in a red sauce. 'You've ruined them!'

'I thought I'd amuse myself, seeing how my credit cards were all taken from me.'

'Your cards?'

'Yes.'

'There must be some mistake.'

'Oh come on Paul, you cancelled them, I've never been so humiliated in all my life.'

'I'll call the bank, I don't know anything about it.'

The next morning Paul found Samantha in the kitchen.

'You're up early', he said.

'I didn't feel well.'

'You've been out of sorts lately, what is it?'

'Nothing.'

'I called the credit card companies and they say there'd been fraudulent activity on your cards, which is why they stopped them.'

'Fraud?'

'It's OK we're covered. They're issuing you with new ones, you'll have to wait a couple of days.'

'So what do I do in the meantime?'

'I'll give you some cash.'

'You didn't cancel my cards?'

'Samantha, I would never do that to you.'

'A couple of days?'

'Yes.'

'All right.'

After Paul had left to go to work, she phoned Jack and got his voicemail.

'Hi darling it's me. Get dressed, I'm coming over and then I'm taking us out to lunch.'

She counted the money Paul had left her and got ready.

Jack stirred as the phone rang in the next room. He could hear Samantha's voice as he rose and pulled his curtains before going to make some coffee.

He played her message and checked the time, realising he was too late to cancel. Her demands and assumptions were beginning to irritate him and he wondered how he could cut himself loose from her.

A letter was waiting for him on his mat as he stepped out of the shower. It contained a notice from the leaseholders that they intended to buy back the flats and they weren't offering much.

It explained he would have to come up with a sum of money or vacate the premises. It was a sum of money he didn't have.

Samantha seemed his best option now.

Samantha needs to be penetrated
Corrupt whore, husband's object.

81

Max was habitually drunk.

The image of Lucinda lying in her blood made the house unbearable to him and he stayed out as much as he could. One afternoon he turned up at Paul's office.

Marching over to his desk he said 'You only told me because you see me as a business rival.'

'Told you what?'

'About Lucinda and Jack.'

'No, Max, I told you as a friend.'

'Is that what you call it?'

'Yes. As a matter of fact, I do.'

Paul stood up and put his hands in his pockets.

'If none of this had happened she might still be alive', Max said.

'You're drunk.'

'That little bastard's fucking your wife, you do know that?'

'Max, you need to sober up.'

'Don't tell me what to do.'

'I understand you're grieving, it's terrible what happened to Lucinda.'

'Do you know what it's like finding your wife dead as you come in? She was butchered!'

'No, I probably don't.'

'And you put up with it.'

'Put up with what?'

'Jack fucking Samantha.'

'No, I don't put up with it, because it isn't happening.'

'I don't know how you can be so calm, everyone knows!'

With that he left and went straight to the nearest pub where he ordered a double whisky.

When Paul removed his hands from his pockets after Max had left, they were shaking so much he had to pour himself a large cognac to still his rage.

Jack Martins opened the front door of his flat.

He peered down the street.

A few minutes later as a black cab drew up he emerged carrying two large suitcases.

He got in and leaned forward.

'Heathrow, please.'

82

Flare and Steele were honing their list of doctors with a history of malpractice.

Steele spotted him.

'There's a guy called Doctor Morris, or should I say Mr. Morris?', she said to Flare. 'Several years ago he was finally struck off after a series of complaints by women patients that he had performed unnecessary hysterectomies on them ended in an investigation that found him guilty. One patient said he'd removed her clitoris.'

'You're joking. He was a private doctor?'

'Yes, his clients were very wealthy. He was Samantha DeLonge's gynaecologist.'

'Sounds like we should pay him a visit. I say we take him by surprise, we haven't got time to call Special Ops.'

'There's more. The woman in question was troubled by a memory she claims to have from when she was under anesthetic.'

'What did he do?'

'It's what he said. She heard him say "This will taste good" as he removed it.'

Their little world is whittled down
Like carved bone.
The Gloss is fading from their lives
Their houses made of glass.

As she shopped Samantha tried Jack's number repeatedly only to get his voicemail. He'd left after lunch saying he had an appointment. She returned later to his flat in irritation. She rang the bell and waited.

Finally Samantha went home and opened a bottle of wine. No one did this to her.

Geoffrey Morris was enjoying a quiet afternoon in his garden.

His roses were looking lush, a warm sun hung overhead and his lawn bore the immaculate look that only an English lawn can.

He sat with a cup of tea and read the paper. The scandals that ended his medical career were long ago and forgotten, and he liked his life. He had no money worries and did as he wished.

The first time the bell rang he ignored it, the second he got up in irritation thinking he'd give whoever was selling something a piece of his mind. The sight of Flare and Steele at the door threw him.

'Geoffrey Morris?', Flare said, holding up his badge.

'Yes.'

'May we come in?'

'What is this about?'

'It would be easier to talk inside.'

'Very well.'

He showed them into the front room.

'We would like to talk to you concerning some recent murders', Flare said.

'Murders?'

'You've probably read about them in the papers.'

He looked from Flare to Steele.

'Are you mad?'

'We need you to come to the station with us, would you do that?'

'No.'

Flare read him his rights, cuffed him, and they escorted him to the car.

83

Geoffrey Morris sat staring resentfully at Flare.

He didn't acknowledge Steele's presence, a facet, she thought, of the latent sexism behind his medical training and also of his personality.

'You like desexing women, Mr. Morris?', she said to him as they opened the interview.

Morris kept his eyes on Flare.

'I was struck off over a misunderstanding, is this the reason you brought me here?'

'A misunderstanding?', Flare said, 'that's not how it looks from here. You repeatedly performed unnecessary operations on a series of women without their consent, effectively ruining their lives.'

'These women, these wealthy playthings of the rich and idle entered my surgery with problems, deep emotional problems I was meant to cure. Do you know how many times I advised psychiatry for them?'

'Maybe it was you who needed it.'

Morris ignored the taunt. It didn't scratch him, and Flare felt he was looking at a man who believed himself to be superior to his clients.

'They asked me to perform operations because

their husbands were cheating on them, because they wanted to have affairs and not get pregnant.'

'So you're saying you never performed an unnecessary operation?'

'I'm saying I worked with the wealthy, and sometimes they asked me to do things which doctors in the NHS wouldn't have done. It's about money, Detective, and I did what they asked, within reason.'

'You were struck off.'

'It happens all the time.'

'We're investigating a series of brutal murders, which you have probably read about in the press.'

'Of course I have read about them.'

'Have you ever performed an operation on someone who wasn't your patient, Mr. Morris?'

'What does that mean?'

'It means have you ever conducted a surgical procedure outside a surgery?'

'No.'

'Let me show you some pictures.'

Flare laid shots of the last victims in front of him. Morris looked at the wounds to Razor and Lucinda Hereford without blinking.

Steele carefully studied his face for a reaction, a giveaway glance, however small, but there was none.

'Yes?', he said, looking at Flare.

'Your handiwork?', Steele said.

He didn't look at her.

'No.'

'Why won't you make eye contact with me, Mr. Morris?', she said.

He turned to her and looked her straight in the eyes. She noticed he had kind eyes, like a benevolent uncle.

'Because, as a modern woman you will have already judged me for the malpractice I was found guilty of, wrongly guilty. I might add as a modern woman you will have made your uneducated and limited mind up and I am wasting my time talking to you because you are as narrow minded as all the bigoted men you feel superior to, simply because feminism has handed you some liberty you do not know how to use or enjoy responsibly. Does that answer your question?'

'You don't like women much, do you, Mr. Morris?', Flare said.

'I don't think anything of them.'

'Do you hate them enough to kill them?'

'Is this all you've got? Because I think I've got nothing further to say until my lawyer gets here.'

He folded his arms and stared at the clock.

Flare put him in a cell until his lawyer arrived.

'He's got some strange views on women', Steele said.

'Doesn't make him the killer, though.'

ETERNAL EROTIC

84

Morris sat with his lawyer, his hands neatly folded on his lap.

'Detective Flare', his lawyer said, 'if you haven't got anything better than the theory that because my client was struck off for some operations performed a long time ago, he is in some way connected to these murders, then I suggest you let him go.'

'I think you're taking revenge on the set of people you served, Mr. Morris', Flare said, 'I think your life fell apart when you were struck off and you are now carrying on with the pathology you'd already started, because you can't help it, because it is a compulsion.'

'The pathology I had already started?'

'Cutting people open.'

'How ridiculous!'

'They took something away from you, didn't they? Your licence to engage in this disease. And now you're doing it to the people who used to pay you.'

'You haven't got a case, I don't think you even have a clue as to who this killer is. But if you don't let me go soon, I will come at you for wrongful arrest.'

Samantha goes shopping, erotic shopping.
Today she is carrying bags, she can see her reflection in them,
They fill the hole left by Jack.
The shops are her haven,
Sometimes she shops online.
She likes Pleasurements and enjoys their Les Jupons De Tess Peek a Boo knickers,
She is on show at the club
Face behind her Sweet Adventure mask,
They know her body
The same way they knew Lucinda's
Behind her Thief Of Love mask.
Samantha has bought a Cadolle Porno chic bra for Jack,
She will let him see her tits above the detail stitched satin.
She wears Guia la Bruna,
She enjoys it against her skin.
Samantha, your citadel is crumbling and you don't even know it.

85

The team assembled by Flare and Steele worked late and Google-searched every reference to the service industry, looking for clues as to what the killer might do to lead him into contact with the Glamour Set. Harvard told them he was convinced the killer wasn't Morris.

'If we were on the right track in our thinking and the killer doesn't work in the medical profession, what other areas would give him access to them?', Flare said to Steele.

'He knows their lives, it's as if he's part of their lives, observing them, but not actually one of them.'

'So what does that indicate?'

'Maybe it's nothing to do with a profession.'

Samantha admired her purchases while standing in front of her full length mirror, putting on some of the new lingerie. She thought what would appeal to Jack. She put on her porno chic bra and Peak a Boo knickers and mooched about the empty house, becoming progressively drunker. She was not going to get in another taxi and go round to Jack, he could come to her. Paul wouldn't be back until late. They wouldn't be interrupted. She rang his number.

'Jack, Samantha, had enough, if you don't come round here today, I'm going to let everyone know about your criminal past and the little disease you've been spreading about.'

She hung up and waited, drinking more wine and drifting. She began to feel cold and slung a silk negligee over her body.

When the bell rang she didn't hesitate in opening the door. She started talking as she did.

'So you thought you'd fucking come.'

As her visitor entered she stopped short.

'You?'

She took a step backwards and was hit so hard in the face by the gloved hand she landed against the banister.

'Samantha, I like your style', he said. He pulled her negligee open and played with her breasts. 'You see beneath my mask. Nice tits, Jack must have enjoyed you. And you do show your arse well in those. The desire of all those men must have been quite an aphrodisiac. I'm sure you used to get wet being watched and wanted like that. Did you get it on your Guia la Bruna panties? A little wetness on your Galatea briefs? You wouldn't have liked your future, you'd get old and men wouldn't want you anymore. You see I know everything about you. I am sure you will taste good.'

Samantha tried to get to her feet but she saw a flash

of something in the air and felt blood running down her stomach. She braced herself against the banisters as he looked her in the face.

'All alone', he said. 'Just you and me, you could have let me watch you. I could have been another watcher, and now it's come to this. I don't need this anymore, Swarovski will be your final fuck, I'll make you a real designer whore.' He removed his mask.

Samantha began to scream as he cut her open, but he silenced her by slicing her throat until all that came out of her mouth were small red bubbles. He inserted the mask inside her vagina. Then he cut off her breasts and placed them in a clear plastic bag which he sealed. He removed her heart and showed it to her and ran his hands inside her until she passed out. He cut the letter G into her neck. Then he poured ashes into the gaping wound in the middle of her chest.

He left by the front door.

86

When the maid arrived the next morning and found her she ran into the front garden screaming.

A neighbour heard her and called the police. The officers who arrived immediately knew this was Flare's case. Maurice Ray was already there when they arrived and he turned away as Steele entered the crime scene.

'How recently was she murdered?', Flare said.

'She was killed late last night', Ray said.

For a few moments Flare and Steele stared at the body before going out for some air.

'Morris was in his cell when this murder was committed', Flare said.

'I know', Steele said.

They drove back to the station where they let Morris go.

Her flesh is particularly sweet,
All the rich food she ate when alive has been absorbed by it and entered into its texture.
She is a wealthy picking,
A quality cut of meat.

Paul DeLonge was at his office when Flare and Steele told him about Samantha's death. He couldn't bring himself to go back to the house.

He booked himself into the Ritz and the next morning went to his office, where he got progressively drunker as the day wore on. He felt he might be next on the list.

That evening he returned to his room and sat staring at the wall until he decided to go out.

He hadn't eaten all day.

He walked to his favourite restaurant.

'He's removed her heart', Frank Norris said to Flare and Steele as they stared at Samantha DeLonge's mutilated body. 'After raping her with a designer mask.'

Back in their office they told Harvard about the latest killing.

'Morris worked for the kind of people being killed', Harvard said.

'What are you saying Don?', Flare said.

'I'm saying that so far you were right in your line of thinking, but you were looking in the wrong place.'

'You mean the killer's someone who is employed by these people?'

'Not necessarily employed, he might serve them.'

'What areas does that throw up?'

'Who would use anatomical parts?', Steele said.

87

She yielded to the cutting.
These wealthy women open so, they are so giving.
She joins the others.
The set stay together now and mingle on a flame.

As Paul DeLonge walked he couldn't shake off the image of Samantha lying butchered in their inviolable home. He needed to keep his strength up and find whoever was behind this. He was angry with the police. He would catch this killer himself and show them up for the incompetents they were. Then he could set about systematically destroying their careers.

Flare's face loomed before him and he imagined burning it in a fire. And as for Steele, she didn't even register as a woman on his radar.

As he was about to enter the restaurant he heard a voice at his shoulder.

'Hello Paul.'

He turned to see a rather dishevelled Max Hereford standing there.

Immediately his sympathies were roused, two fellow widowers standing face to face in the street.

'How are you?'

'Not good. I heard about Samantha.'

'What is going on?'

'It's as if our entire world is under assault.'

'I was about to eat, would you join me?'

'That would be nice.'

They entered Le Feu and sat at a table in the corner. It was a table they'd used many times before. They ordered and consumed a bottle of Petrus as they waited for their dinner to be served.

'Who is this guy?', Max said, his eyes glazing over.

'I don't know and it's obvious the police don't have a clue, but one thing's for sure, I'm going to find out and I'm going to take the law into my own hands.'

'Be careful.'

'My wife's lying dead, so is yours, don't you feel angry?'

'Of course I do, what I'm saying is that this isn't the Wild West and vigilante style killings don't go down well with the modern constabulary, they'll send you away for it, and is he worth it?'

'Samantha is, and besides, I'm not talking about a vigilante style killing.'

'What then?'

'I'll pay someone, a professional to torture him and take him out.'

Max took a long swig on the Petrus as the waiter brought their hors d'oeuvres.

'Two game pies. Enjoy.'

Paul sank his knife into it, crunching the pastry and lifting a heavy forkful of soft moist meat to his stained lips. He swigged another glass back and ordered a second bottle.

'He's generous with his meat', Max said.

'Marcus is one of the best chefs in London.'

'This is incredibly fresh.'

'It always is.'

'He has a fantastic supplier.'

'Especially where game is concerned', Paul said.

'He's probably cooked this himself.'

The second bottle came and Paul poured them both a glass.

'Here's to finding out who killed our wives', he said.

'Yes.'

They talked, brooding over their losses as they drank.

Paul felt himself relax. He thought about returning home later. Then he remembered he was booked into the Ritz and how his world had changed.

The second course arrived.

'One liver, one casserole. Enjoy.'

The conversation lulled a little while they ate, a strange calm coming over them both.

They ordered cognacs and sat reminiscing.

'You know, our set is unique, we need to protect it', Paul said.

'What against, serial killers?', Max said.

'More than that, keep the little people out.'

'Yes.'

'It's because of us that people like Marcus exist. I've nothing against that, what I'm talking about is the intrusion by people who don't understand, who don't even share our value system and the impact they have on our lives.'

'Like the police?'

'Like the police.'

'I want to find Jack Martins', Max said.

'Tell me if you do.'

They finished their cognacs and Paul paid.

Outside they said their goodbyes.

'I'm not going to let this matter settle, Max.'

'Let's speak.'

'Of course.'

'We're the only two left.'

Paul walked back to the Ritz and Max hailed a taxi. He gave the driver Jack Martins's address. When he got there he kicked the door in swiftly and went in. It was dark inside and he toured the empty rooms looking for a clue. He heard a noise at his shoulder.

'So you're here', he said, turning round.

88

Don Harvard made a breakthrough.

'He's enacting Isaiah 3:24', he said.

'You mean the killings refer to the Bible?', Flare said.

'"Instead of fragrance there will be a stench, instead of a sash, a rope, instead of well-dressed hair, baldness, instead of fine clothing, sackcloth, instead of beauty, branding." That's the passage and it relates to what the killer has done to the female victims.'

'He smashed a bottle of perfume when he killed Martha Fornalski', Flare said.

'He hanged Sandra Gould by a rope', Steele said.

Don nodded.

'He shaved Anne Lacey's head and he covered Lucinda Hereford with a sackcloth. He is removing their glamorous lifestyles as he kills them.'

'So it's religiously motivated', Flare said.

'It is. With Samantha DeLonge it's the ashes that accompany the sackcloth. He poured them into the wound he made when he removed her heart. Sexuality and religion are connected for him.'

'Forensics say the ash is burnt clothing', Flare said.

'It's more than likely he burnt some of the lingerie

his female victims wore. He is turning Glamour to ash, he is burning their sexuality.'

'What are the letters on Lucinda Hereford and Samantha DeLonge?', Steele said.

'The A on Lucinda's neck is for Aubade, famous for it's Boite A Desir.'

'What does that mean?', Flare said.

'Drunk With Desire. It uses names like Forbidden Lesson for its lingerie.'

'What about Samantha DeLonge?', Flare said.

'G for Guia La Bruna.'

'Were they wearing these brands when they were killed?', Flare said.

'Lucinda was in her nightie, I wouldn't be surprised if her wardrobe contains Aubade. Samantha was wearing peek a boo knickers by Les Jupons De Tess and a porno chic bra by Cadolle, who was the inventor of the modern bra. Again she will own Guia La Bruna. The killer is making a point of saying he knows their preferred lingerie. He is obsessed with brands, he feels branded.'

Flare touched the side of his face and looked away as Harvard said this.

Later that day Flare searched through every connection they'd come up with concerning what the killer might do. The sense that they weren't looking for a doctor seemed right. He was hungry and finding it hard to think when he went down to the police café. The sandwiches were gone and all that was left was a stew which looked overcooked. He sat and ate, digging his fork into the meat. It was tough and he chewed for a long time on the first mouthful before looking for a steak knife and cutting it into smaller pieces. That was when he made a connection.

Back upstairs he said to Steele and Harvard 'He's a chef.'

'That's a possibility', Harvard said, 'someone who is used to handling meat and who knows how to cut it.

'So who?', Steele said.

'We find out which restaurants they used and check out every chef working there', Flare said.

The cleaners did a good job.

Once the police had finished with the murder scene they removed every trace of the attack on Samantha and Paul returned home.

After a few minutes he poured himself a whisky and left for the office where he made frequent visits to the bar.

He poured the blood and guts into the dish he'd prepared earlier. He mused on the hidden properties of leaves.

His hands were stained with the fluids and he rinsed some of the small pieces of skin away under the tap, watching them swirl and run down the plughole.

He fetched some organs from a jar and slurped them into the mixture, stirring them in.

Then he took several of the thin slices he'd cut earlier and fricasseed them in oil, watching them sizzle and hiss on the skillet.

Behind him the figure of Christ stood like an admonishing parent and he turned and looked at it before returning to his task. His clothes were starched white and immaculate, unmarked by any of the activities he engaged in.

He placed it all lovingly on a plate, adding some decoration at the side.

89

At the station Flare suddenly lit up.

They'd been searching through the histories of the chefs who would have exposure to the Glamour Set, chefs with direct contact with the victims, and one name stood out.

'Marcus Floren runs a restaurant they all went to', he said.

Don Harvard looked up.

'He has a good pedigree.'

'Yes, and he may just be our man.'

'What else have you got on him?' Steele said.

'I'm running a search now.'

He wiped down the work surfaces. Alone in his restaurant he ensured every spot of grease and blood was removed, replaced by the smell of chemicals.

To him this was an ending, a ritual transformation of the meat he let others digest. He thought of them, the trophies he'd fetched from their set entering their systems and slowly altering them. They became the thing he made them.

He reached into the cupboard and looked at the remaining jars.

He'd preserved them and now they were part of his process, part of what he was choosing to turn them into.

The flesh seemed endless, a pathway of routes from the abyss and into the minds and souls of others, the lives he was excluded from and served.

They were so beneath him, he wanted to inflict greater levels of pain and cruelty on them, and his mouth filled with a rush of saliva at the thoughts his psyche yielded. He wanted to penetrate these women with sharp instruments, to hear their cries, summoned from death's doorway, to watch them in the place they never dared to access before their husbands, who only got that small and acrid part of them.

He knew what dark secrets their sexuality held as he cut them. They opened like bleeding flowers into the pathways of this violation.

He was stealing their husbands' property and considered himself a magician thief, a changer of the corrupt into the worthy. As they ate one another at his restaurant, as they sat at his tables vaunting their shallow sense of superiority, worthless as the notes they gave him, he cooked them in his steaming skillet and served them up whole and ready for their own consumption.

Eating was about taking on the identity of the thing you were eating.

He'd known that as he studied to be a chef. That was the reason he'd chosen to become a chef. Power was wrapped up in eating as surely as in the orders of a king.

His clients didn't see that they were in his power.

He considered the ways he could prepare and present the final specimens of meat.

By adding the two remaining members of the set he would give a certain piquancy to the dish he had in mind.

THE WATCHFUL EYES
OF STRANGERS

90

There are doubles in my world
My Mirror is made of steel.

Flare looked at Marcus Floren's background.

'There are no previous criminal convictions or even arrests', he said.

'No', Harvard said, 'but his medical record says it all. He was sectioned as a young man for schizophrenia, although I think the diagnosis only goes skin deep.'

'Are you saying they misdiagnosed him?'

'I'm saying that most diagnoses that point to schizophrenia are using a blanket term, a way of psychiatrists saying, "this guy's seriously ill and we need to keep him in here a long time, long enough to find a regime of medication that stops his psychosis dead in its tracks".'

'No shit.'

'If you read different definitions of schizophrenia, they clash. Psychiatry contains many contradictions surrounding it.'

Steele looked at the medical record.

'In his sessions with the psychiatrist he was talking about eating his sister', she said.

'I know. There are more notes on him I want to look at.'

'They diagnosed early stages of cannibalism.'

'He's using their body parts to attack the set. He's feeding them each other', Harvard said.

His comment left Flare and Steele in stunned silence.

Flare got a couple of Special Ops officers. They raced to Le Feu.

Flare had driven past many times and watched the idle wealthy customers eating, thinking of his policeman's paycheck.

The windows were dark when they got there and they tried the back entrance. The restaurant was empty.

In his private kitchen he prepared tomorrow's dishes.

He felt and placed each organ within the thick marinade he'd prepared earlier, the signature dish which made him famous.

He stirred each body part into the mixture and let it settle, watching it sink down to the bottom. Then he removed his white uniform and turned to the statue of Christ.

Blood and guts adhered to its surface like the issue of a bomb blast.

Flare, Steele and Harvard were discussing how to catch him.

'He got out of section and never returned', Harvard said. 'He tricked the psychiatrists and led a normal life, long enough to get to become one of the top chefs in London.'

'So what are you saying Don?', Flare said.

'There's something here that doesn't add up. He was too able to convince them he was well, too able to carry on a normal life without medication.'

'Usually someone with that history would need long term medication to be able to function at all, right?', Steele said.

'Absolutely, and Marcus Floren stopped taking his many years ago. There is no record of any prescriptions for him after he left the mental institution.'

'So what can we deduce from that?'

'It's hard to say, Jackson, but either he wasn't that bad to begin with or there was something else wrong with him entirely.'

'Like what?'

'One of the psychiatrists diagnosed multiple personality disorder, but the others didn't agree, say he was right?'

'If there are different Marcuses, are you saying one of them might not be mentally ill?'

'Exactly. With multiples, genuine multiples, which are extremely rare, in the early stages of the illness there may be a dominant personality with mental problems. It draws attention to itself, gets itself sectioned. The others get angry, gang up on it so to speak, and one takes over in order to protect the disease.'

'Say that is the case, which one took over here?'

'The psychopath.'

'Who's doing the killings.'

'Right.'

'Now we just face one problem', Flare said, 'where to find him. There's no registered address for Marcus Floren.'

91

He faced him with the whip.

They looked so alike, twin pieces of a puzzle no one could crack. Their words merged with each other's resonance, like some symbolic utterance.

He lacerated his brother's flesh, bringing the blood rush that sated him there within the dance of their identities, the two of them enacting the ancient drama.

'The cross has borne you upon its wheel', he said. 'The cross is turning within the folds of time.'

The other looked down at him, the mirror of the separate and dual selves locked in the room.

'We are raising the energies of all the fallen', Marcus said, 'we are taking the lives of the selfish and greedy away from the tables where they eat themselves, always at rancour with the truth. We were always brothers and are the true enactment of the secret scriptures, of which they do not know.'

He dropped the whip and untied him there and let his brother go.

Harvard found it.

He searched through the birth records and saw the

piece of evidence that made sense of it all. 'Marcus Floren had an identical twin, also named Marcus.'

'What are the odds of that?', Flare said.

'I've done some background checks on the mother, Mabel Thomson, who renamed herself Hortensia Floren and she was schizophrenic. She was obsessed with Roman history. Hortensia was a wealthy Roman woman who wore exquisite jewellery and owned slaves.'

'Sounds like one of Marcus Floren's victims', Steele said. 'Could he have known this about his mother?'

'It's possible he found out.'

'What about the father?', Flare said.

'The father was unknown. The two boys didn't see their mother after the age of two, she committed suicide. They were raised together in foster homes before one of them began to display signs of mental illness as a teenager.'

'Which one?', Flare said.

'Not the killer I think.'

'If they're both called Marcus how do you know which one went crazy?', Steele said.

'With identical twins you usually have a dominant one, in this case it's the killer. There's a note from a psychiatrist about Marcus Floren's obsession that his real name was Kester Floren. The note reads "the patient claims his brother has renamed him, which is further evidence of his religious mania". But he was wrong. Marcus Floren the patient was telling the truth. I think the dominant twin, the killer, renamed his brother to differentiate himself from him and to assign him a role.'

'Being what?', Flare said.

'To bear his Christ obsession, Kester means "Bearing Christ" or "Christ carrier".'

'What does Marcus mean?', Steele said.

'Dedicated to Mars', Harvard said, 'and Floren means flowering.'

'Sounds like Mabel Thomson wanted to unleash war in her children', Flare said.

'She got it', Steele said.

'Marcus, or Kester let's call him', Harvard said, 'was sectioned with schizophrenia, not his brother, the killer. I would guess the reason Kester got out of the section was that Marcus switched with him at a visit. He then convinced the psychiatrists he was all right. He's no doubt been looking after Kester ever since.'

'How long was he sectioned for?', Flare said.

'Six months. I estimate from reading the psychiatrist's notes that Marcus switched with Kester after four months.'

'Why do you say that?', Flare said.

'Because the initial notes on Marcus Floren state he was categorically showing signs of schizophrenia and being unresponsive to therapy. He was on a heavy regime of antipsychotic drugs and medicating him was all they seemed able to do to arrest his delusions. Then two months before he was released he began to ask about joining a therapy group. According to the therapist he was cooperative and focused. The switch is uncharacteristic of someone who is schizophrenic.'

'So Kester goes in and Marcus comes out.'

'That's what I think.'

'Who looked after Kester while Marcus was inside?', Steele said.

'The sister Catherine Floren had a council flat. Records show around two months before she disappeared she claimed carer's benefits for looking after her brother.'

'So Marcus goes in, and takes two months to convince the psychiatrists he's well', Flare said.

Harvard nodded.

'One of the final entries in the psychiatric notes reads "The patient may have suffered an aberrational episode. He is able to integrate in ways he was not previously."'

'They're not both doing the killings?', Flare said.

'No. What they have is the perfect embodiment of a schizophrenic split. I've never come across it before. It doesn't exist in any text book.'

'What does that mean Don?', Flare said.

'Marcus is doing the killing, Kester's schizophrenia can bear his illness for him. Usually the split is internal and breaks at some point, rendering the sufferer ill enough to get put away. But this is on the outside, there are actually two of them and they embody a dynamic which could keep them going indefinitely. Together they are a perfect channelling system for any guilt or dysfunction that might undermine the main enterprise.'

'Being murder?', Flare said.

'Right. Also we have the explanation for the Isaiah enactment in Kester's psychiatric notes. He and Marcus attended a Jesuit school. A priest there had a predilection for boys and was later arrested for taking indecent photographs of them. He branded Kester's genitals with I 3:24. Kester told his psychiatrist that "he branded me and my brother".'

'So Marcus brands his victims with the initial of their favourite designer lingerie and enacts the passage from Isaiah', Flare said.

'Why don't we check out an address for Kester Floren?', Steele said. 'There can't be many people with the name Floren.'

They did and found a flat in Kensington registered to him.

As they drove there they wondered what blood bath awaited them at this haunt, what victims' body parts or other horrors this killer lived with, as if a part of the decor of the place in which he carried out his strange visitations to himself.

92

The Special Ops officers accompanied them. They battered the door down and ascended a brightly lit staircase slowly, carrying their MP5 submachine guns and their holstered Glock 17s. At the top of the stairs they entered a room with two doors off it. Blood flecked the walls and carpet. Christ's face stared at them from the floor and an assortment of whips lay on a table at the centre of the room.

'It smells like an abattoir in here', Steele said, opening a window.

Flare heard the sound of someone moving in the next room. He slowly pushed the door open.

There in the half light a man stood dressed in a loin cloth wiping blood from his face. He was covered in cuts and wounds and moved towards Flare.

The armed officers kept their guns trained on him.

'Marcus Floren, I am arresting you for murder.'

He looked at Flare and said 'Are you come to remove the cross from Golgotha?'

Flare cuffed him while Steele tried the handle of the other door.

'It's locked. I think you have Kester there', she said.

'He's entered his secret kitchen', Kester said.

They kicked the door in. In a steel room Marcus Floren was eating ravenously. He lifted his fork and chewed what looked like tripe.

As the officers kept him in their sights Flare cuffed him.

Marcus Floren looked up at them with calm eyes.

'It's too late, I've eaten the dish whereof they were made, all of them, and Mr. Glamour is born.'

93

At the station Flare and Steele began their interview of Marcus Floren while they kept Kester in a cell. Steele noted his looks with interest: bronzed, blue eyes, handsome in a disturbing way. She wondered why she hadn't expected this, as if he would have to be ugly to watch and kill women the way he did. The interview itself made her question her own attraction to certain types of men. Kester looked just like his brother, except his face bore the marks of a suffering that seemed absent on Marcus's face. Kester's eyes wandered as he spoke, Marcus's were focused, like two pinpoints of light.

'Marcus Floren, you are the killer of Larry Fornalski, Martha Fornalski, Martin Gould, Sandra Gould, Anne Lacey, Razor, Lucinda Hereford and Samantha DeLonge', Flare said.

Marcus spoke emotionlessly now, as if he was viewing a piece of film.

'I was their chef, they all went to Le Feu and I served them, made signature dishes for them. But they didn't see me as part of their set.'

'Did you kill them?'

'I cooked them. The wives flirted. They would wear

revealing clothes and want to be noticed, to be seen.'

'This is part of your imagination', Steele said, 'in your sick mind you thought these women were flirting with you. Is that why you killed them?'

'I pity you,' Marcus Floren said. 'I watched your investigation, knew all the wrong steps you took, and now you have me yet you don't. In a few days there will be nothing you can do.'

'Why did you do it?', Steele said.

'Exclusion. You felt excluded didn't you Detective Flare? Left out of a world that looks down its nose at you, and you Detective Steele, you want things your life doesn't give you, I can see it.'

'You are a successful chef. Why kill?', Flare said.

'They denied me their nudity.'

'So you wanted to sleep with the women, they rejected you and you killed them', Steele said. 'We know what happened to your genitals as a boy.'

'Do you?'

'That's why you branded them', Flare said.

'Branding is a complicated matter. There are the designer brands these women were obsessed by, I knew every one. I saw them wear their Versace dresses and I knew what lingerie they wore when they were alone or getting fucked by Jack Martins.'

'You're impotent, is that it?', Steele said.

'No I'm not, I'm King in a world of voyeurs. You like watching don't you Detective Steele? I may have watched you. I am good at it. You alone with a man on your bed, how do you like to do it? Then you're of no interest to me. I bet you don't own a single designer brand. Maybe a repro, some cheap piece of clothing you try to look sexy in.'

'You were marked by that priest and you wanted to mark someone. That's why you enacted the passage from Isaiah in your killings', Steele said.

'You probably think that I can't talk about it, that the trauma is so bad. The priest used to watch the boys in the shower. He approached me for sex and I refused. The next day he decided to punish me. He was unable to tell the difference between me and my brother. He took us into his room and branded both of us with the passage from Isaiah. He was deformed you see, hideous. He hated beauty but wanted it.'

'Like you? You hated the beautiful women you killed.'

'I am not deformed.'

'These women wouldn't have you, would they?', Steele said.

'They were whores.'

'No they weren't. They rejected you and you killed them.'

'Do you know what the password was?'

'What password?', Flare said.

'Vergucci. It's what they used to keep the others out, I found out, but by then I had lost interest in going there, I'd seen it all, caught them on my S2 Leica. I have quite a collection of pictures Detective Flare, that should mean something to you. I have money. I find information. I watch and I capture them on film.'

'You watched them because you couldn't have them', Steele said.

'They were watched by everyone. You don't know about the Glamour Club do you? Do you remember the ring I stuffed down Martin Gould's throat? Remember the letters on it?'

'GC', Flare said.

'I knew about the Glamour Club, the leather lined rooms where they paraded their wives naked. The men and women who frequented Le Feu loved my food. They also had unusual sexual habits. They treated their wives as property and they would allow other business associates to watch them walk naked among the private rooms of their exclusive club.'

'You're saying the people you were killing were part of some voyeuristic club?', Flare said.

'Yes. I will give you the address. The club housed designer goods of all descriptions. The leather walls shone in the lurid crimson light as the naked and clothed mingled. The letters GC were all that were visible on the huge black door of the Mayfair house. The limousines that drew up had blacked out windows and the men and women who got out wore masks.

These were the sexual masques of the Glamour Set. The wives liked to be the object of voyeurism. They came out in lingerie. The letters I cut into their necks were the brands they wore. They'd strip and walk round naked while their faces remained hidden. Since they felt they were on display in their marriages, little more than appendages for their husbands, they obtained some measure of sexual gratification from exposing themselves to the watchful eyes of their husbands' business rivals. The men who watched them enjoyed guessing who they were. They would hire models to mingle with their wives to make the guessing harder. There was never any sex. Afterwards they would dress in their own private changing rooms and dine with faces shown.'

'So they wouldn't let you attend?', Flare said.

'No. I wasn't good enough for them. When I heard about the Glamour Club from a drunk Samantha DeLonge, I approached Brian Samson. I told him I'd like to join. "Sorry, it's only for us", he said, laying a hand on my shoulder. "How do I get in?", I said. "You don't." I asked him what the rules of membership were. "You have to be part of the set", he said. "So what am I?", I said. "You're a fine chef". I knew then what I would do. I would be the chef of them.'

'How do you know so much about it?'

'I paid one of the waiters to take pictures. They hired Anne Lacey to go there to mingle with their wives, to show her snatch. I heard Razor arguing with Anne outside when she left the night she went there, he was furious with her. I knew them from Le Feu. She was a cheap whore, she used to flirt with everyone at my restaurant. My restaurant, and I wasn't good enough for them. And so I watched them. I was interested in photography when I was younger, considered it as a career before I discovered cooking. I took their pictures, when they were naked and alone at home and

I saw what they showed to men they knew through their husbands' business deals. You see, these women were no better than whores. They liked to be watched and they shared lovers. The Glamour Set is the world of mirrors. I was the Mirror Man but now I am more.'

'Why did you brand their necks?', Steele said.

'A message to the Set that I knew. They would wear chokers on their necks when they went to the Glamour Club. The veins stood out beneath them, most arousing, like an animal that is about to be slaughtered. As a trainee chef I visited an abattoir. There is great beauty in the startled terror in an animal's eyes as it is led to the processing line. The halter restrains them much as the chokers on the erotic necks of the wives did. Detective Steele you look uncomfortable. Is there something you do in private, something sexual that you keep hidden from your colleagues?'

'Why did you remove their organs?', Flare said.

'I wanted to control the food chain. Eating your victims is the ultimate source of power, you absorb them into you. I fed them to each other. The men ate their whores. I was a chef to them. So I used them for my dishes. They were eating each other and they didn't know it. I branded them and fed them to each other. When you eat someone their memories are transferred to you. I wanted their memories, I relive their nights at the Glamour Club, I have reels of film in my head of their sex lives, I can hear Martha Fornalski scream as she achieved orgasm when Jack Martins fucked her. I can see Sandra Gould masturbating and hear the noises she made as she came. I live in the Glamour Club. I see it through all their eyes. I know that Larry Fornalski used to rape Martha. He used whores and would visit one who was a compulsive cleaner. He would go to this whore who used to clean all the time.'

Flare and Steele exchanged glances.

'I'm right aren't I? You know about this. You see what I've done isn't ordinary killing. I've taken on their identities, all that Glamour. There's something else you don't know, you will find out when you realise your laws are powerless to stop me, that you may imprison me but I will escape.'

'You're just a sick man who was abused as a child and took revenge on a crowd that rejected you', Steele said.

She looked at him then and his eyes fixed on hers. She thought she saw beneath the pupils some mechanism at work, watchful and cold, as if his eyes were cameras. As she held his stare she felt as though he was absorbing her. And she caught a flicker, as if his lenses were made of glass and a shutter had taken her image.

Marcus Floren leaned forward until his face was inches from Steele's. She held her position.

'Aren't you a little sick Detective Steele? How high do you like to get when you achieve orgasm and how far do you push the law for your sexual needs?'

His eyes were focused on her throat and Steele could feel a vein swell and throb there. She was reminded of the interview with Jack Martins when he looked at her with all the knowing of a serial seducer and she felt small and unwelcome. She thought how this might have led her further into the sexual darkness with Mark and how she was still under Allen's shadow. She wanted a line between her and Marcus Floren.

'What else don't we know?', she said.

'There are a few surprises in store for you. Do you like kidneys Detectives Flare and Steele?'

'Not particularly', Flare said.

'Ask my brother what I did yesterday.'

94

They took Marcus back to his cell.

'Kester may be an accomplice to the killings', Flare said. 'Let's interview him.'

He sat there peacefully looking at them.

'Do you know what your brother has been doing?', Flare said.

'He is a chef.'

'Have you ever helped him?'

'No he always worked alone. Ever since he ate our sister.'

'What did he do yesterday?', Flare said.

'He impregnated Christ.'

'Did you see it?', Steele said.

'I am Christ. I placed my seed within the womb and he made the dish whereof he ate to bear the mystic pregnancy he designed.'

'What do you make of what he told us?', Flare said to Harvard.

'Marcus Floren's cannibalism began when he ate his sister. His cannibalism is heavily ritualised, involving elements of his distorted religion.'

'What about their mental states?'

'Kester is insane', Harvard said. 'Marcus is a psychopath and he knows what he is doing.'

'Is Kester aware that his brother has been killing?', Steele said.

'I think he's beyond acknowledging such things.'

'So we have another Gertrude Miller in Kester in terms of how the courts would view him', Flare said.

'Yes. And I don't think he is guilty of any crimes.'

'Let's re-interview Marcus', Flare said.

95

'Your brother said you impregnated Christ yesterday', Steele said.

'I am more than a chef. My brother ejaculated into Lucinda Hereford's womb and I cooked it with Samatha DeLonge's breasts, a perfect accompaniment wouldn't you say? I made a signature dish out of the Glamour Set.'

'Is that what you were eating when we arrested you?', Flare said.

'Yes, you were too late you see. He is being born and I am he.'

'Who?', Flare said.

'Mr. Glamour. Vergucci.'

96

Flare and Steele paid a visit to Max Hereford. There was no response at his house and at his office they were informed he hadn't been seen all day. Efforts to contact him by phone proved fruitless.

They found Paul DeLonge at his office and told him they had made an arrest.

'Who?', he said.

'The chef Marcus Floren', Flare said.

'Marcus? That's impossible, why would he be killing us?'

'He felt rejected by the Glamour Club', Flare said.

Paul DeLonge looked away. He stood and poured himself a cognac.

'Are you sure he's the killer?', he said.

'We are. Can you tell us about the Glamour Club?'

Paul DeLonge nodded and sat down.

'We met every week, entering by separate doors, one each side of the building. The women entered at the back, the men at the front. We had a password, Vergucci, to ensure no one tricked their way in. The waiters who served us were the best paid in London, since we valued discretion. We would wait in the men's room, drinking, and watch the wives enter masked.

Then they would take their lingerie off. Sex was not permitted at the club, nor were outsiders. The women enjoyed the thrill of being watched. They were aroused by the watchfulness of those they knew, seeing who enjoyed their nudity. There was a guessing game the men would play, trying to identify which wife had shaved, which not, trying to measure the size and shape of breasts against those imagined beneath designer clothes. The women would discuss which of their friends' husbands liked them. It was a show, and the wives were the spectacle. Naked, hidden, exposed and aroused, they would return to their homes and go to bed with their husbands who saw the fleeting forms of their wives' friends as they entered them. The following day the wives would treat themselves to some new clothes. We enjoyed knowing our wives were so desired.'

'What has happened to the club?', Flare said.

'There are none of us left, it is empty. The property is owned by me and Max Hereford.'

'Can I have the address?'

'22 Hertford Street.'

Flare and Steele drove there and entered with the key Paul DeLonge gave them. They found it much as Marcus Floren had described, a club rich with the paraphernalia of erotica. A lot of money had gone into it, and the empty corridors reeked of the covert activities of the wealthy. They toured the rooms, seeing how the arrangement would work.

'It's interesting', Flare said, 'no mirrors.'

'You'd think they'd have some, especially when you consider how into watching they were.'

'The mirrors were the men, seeing desire in their faces. These women needed to be watched, here they knew they were.'

Lingerie catalogues by Damaris, Aubade, Guia La Bruna and Bordelle lay on antique tables.

Versace and Gucci accessories filled the shelves that lined one wall.

'The women would have changed in here', Flare said, entering a room with benches and a wardrobe with hangers.

'Then they went through into this room', Steele said, 'they undressed and walked around naked.'

At the end of a long corridor that was lined with red leather was another room.

'This is the kitchen', Flare said.

Steele tried the handle of the final door.

'This is where they ate afterwards', she said.

'It feels like a brothel.'

'Reminds me of Gertrude Miller.'

'A wealthier version. Interesting Brian Samson wanted her.'

As they returned to the main room Steele noticed a Gucci handbag on a table. It was a Soho large shoulder bag with embossed interlocking G and tassels.

'It looks like someone left this', she said, picking it up.

She peered inside and dropped it.

'What is it?', Flare said.

She waited for him to find out.

'Half a heart, I'd say it's Samantha DeLonge's', he said.

Just then a mobile phone pulsed into the room. It was a Versace purple rock touch phone from the Lacquer collection. Flare saw it flashing over on one of the Guia La Bruna catalogues. He went over and answered it.

'I see you found the Glamour Club whore phone. You found her heart did you?', Marcus Floren said.

97

He was calm in the interview room. Steele noticed something different about him, a look she hadn't discerned before, some sparkle of triumph in his eyes.

'Marcus Floren we are charging you with multiple murders', Flare said. 'You have the right to a lawyer.'

'I don't need one. I made my call to the mobile phone at the Glamour Club. Because you see this is beyond crime, this is an art. Do you know what the whore phone was for? The husbands would call the models on it.'

'How did you get access to the Glamour Club?', Flare said.

'I got keys off one of the waiters. This was after I decided to eat them.'

Flare and Steele stepped outside the interview room to consult Don Harvard.

'Is he insane?', Flare said.

'I think he knows what he's done which makes him morally responsible.'

'He doesn't care about the criminal process or the fact that he's going away for life.'

'There are many theories about cannibalism', Don said. 'They are delusional but delusions are powerful.

Marcus Floren may believe he is beyond the law because he has eaten his victims.'

'What do you think?'

'He's kidding himself.'

They went back to the interview room.

As they sat down Steele noticed it again, a look on Marcus's face, both alien and seductive, that didn't seem to belong there. He reminded her of someone else. It wasn't until Marcus made his final revelation that she realised who it was he reminded her of.

'There are still two missing parties', he said.

'Are you saying you've killed more people?', Flare said.

'I followed him in the taxi and met him at the airport. He thought I was returning from a flight, I had a suitcase. He was going to leave and start again. He was the Glamour Man the wives all screwed, he had the look, he was branded gigolo, a pure piece of masculine sex. I offered him work, and he took it. He wanted to regain admittance to the set. I took him to my flat to show him what I had in mind. I have his mind.'

'Who are you talking about?', Flare said.

As he said it Steele pushed her chair backwards.

'Jack Martins.'

'You're saying you killed him', Flare said.

'I am.'

'What did you do with the body?'

Marcus Floren leant towards Flare.

'It's all in the DNA. Most of him has been eaten by the customers at Le Feu. I took the best bit for myself. I fricasseed it with the finest ingredients. He was the one they wanted, he had access to the wives. Even Steele desired him. You will find the rest of him at my flat. I now have his appeal.'

'Who else have you killed?', Flare said.

'Max Hereford. I was at Jack Martins's flat, he told me before I killed him he had pictures of the wives. He was trying to save his life. I didn't find any. Max Hereford turned up. I sliced him open. After he'd eaten Lucinda's flesh. I watched as he and Paul DeLonge ate their wives in my restaurant. I saved a piece of Samantha's heart for you. She tastes good in my gravy. I use dry cider and walnuts.'

'Where's Max Hereford's body?'

'In Jack Martins's flat.'

Flare and Steele searched Marcus Floren's flat first. Al Groper was there gathering evidence. When Steele opened the fridge in the kitchen she saw Jack Martins's head on the first shelf. His eyes stared at her like two ruined gemstones in a broken casing. Flare peered over her shoulder.

'The sick bastard decapitated him. And ate his brains', he said.

They drove to Jack Martins's flat followed by Al Groper.

Max Hereford lay on Jack Martins's bed. He had been cut open and his organs removed.

As they were leaving Flare turned to Groper and said 'I haven't seen Maurice Ray in a while'.

'Haven't you heard?', Groper said.

'Heard what?'

'He got married.'

'I hope he and his boyfriend are happy', Steele said.

'Boyfriend?', Groper said. 'He married a stunning looking woman, I think he was just fussy that's all.'

Steele bit her lip and turned her back to Groper.

They stepped outside and she said to Flare 'Max Hereford must have known Jack Martins had screwed his wife.'

'It got him killed', Flare said.

'He's ended up on the gigolo's bed.'

'Your lip's bleeding.' He watched Steele put her finger to it. 'It seems Marcus Floren wasn't content eating the wives, he started to eat the husbands.'

98

As Flare and Steele were leaving the station they bumped into Frank Norris.

'We have the killer', Flare said.

'No more mutilations then', Norris said.

'Not unless there's another one out there.'

'Who is he?'

'Marcus Floren the chef.'

'Makes you wonder what you eat when you do go out.'

He walked away and Steele watched him pass along the corridor, his pony tail hanging over his collar.

That evening she found Mark waiting for her outside her flat.

She let him in and looked at him and thought of the sexual journey she'd undertaken after Allen raped her. She knew she had to stop it and that if she became addicted it would be harder.

Mark began to touch her and she took his hand.

'I don't want to do this', she said.

'You do.'

He forced her onto the bed and she was back with Allen in her Mini feeling used and dirty as she saw the years open inside her like a bleeding wound. The wound had Marcus Floren's face in it and she wanted to disentangle herself, feeling as though her flesh was caught in barbed wire. Mark had his hand inside her panties and she kicked him and got the cuffs.

As she shackled him to the bed she knew she was not the same woman who had craved sexual darkness a few weeks before, that being a cop had altered a path she'd started to go down.

'I am going to let you go', she said, 'and when I do I want you to leave.'

'What's changed?'

'My job has changed me.'

'You're saying you don't want more?'

'I am.'

She uncuffed him and Mark stood up and looked at her. She held his gaze and he left her flat.

And in that moment she knew Flare was all right, that whatever his burden was it was no danger to her. That together they had solved a case that had shown her where to draw the line.

MIRROR IMAGE

99

At Marcus Floren's flat Flare and Steele found a collection of pictures of the Glamour Set taken by him. They were good shots of the wives undressing and in their lingerie. Flare found it hard looking at them. Their surreptitious nature evoked unpleasant memories in him.

Don Harvard was at the station when they got back.

'It's almost as if nothing matters to Marcus Floren, he's got what he wanted', Flare said.

'He believes he has taken on the identities of the Glamour Set. That is what you are seeing', Harvard said.

'What will happen in prison when he is unable to feed his cannibalism?', Steele said.

'He will probably start to fall apart.'

'Right now he seems unaware of what is happening around him', Flare said.

'He feels he has taken back what the priest and rejection by the Glamour Set removed.'

They interviewed him again.

'Is there anything else you want to tell us?', Flare said.

'No, but you will see that I will not be imprisoned, for I live in the world of doubles and there are two.'

'Two what?'

'My Mirror is unbreakable, you will see.'

'Why didn't you kill Paul DeLonge?', Flare said.

'I plan to, I have his wife's memories. I know all his weaknesses.'

'You won't be doing any killing where you're going.'

'I won't be going there. Don't you know Mr. Glamour wanders the streets at night?'

100

Paul DeLonge would hear noises at night and wake thinking he heard Samantha moving about the house. He would find empty bottles of wine when he rose in the morning, bottles he didn't remember drinking. In the absence of his set he felt diminished, as if Marcus Floren had won. He craved strange foods.

One morning some pictures arrived in the mail.

They were of Samantha and Jack Martins. He stared at her naked body as Martins made love to his wife and he reached for rage to find it swallowed by grief. It was her face that troubled him the most. She looked happy and he knew he had never seen that look during their married life, as if he had been wed to a stranger. Some of the pictures showed Jack Martins making love to her gently, some were rougher, and he saw the shadow of desire on his wife's face and felt redundancy clutch his heart with cold fingers. He wondered if to be a successful lover you had to shed your identity at the door in the same way the wives shed their lingerie at the Glamour Club. He considered how other men had seen her naked and the necessity for control in his character, and a small leaf unfolded inside him. Jack Martins had access to her in ways he didn't. Paul felt watched by a world he didn't belong to.

In the ensuing weeks as Marcus Floren awaited trial the leaf inside Paul DeLonge grew and he could hear it crackle at night. It seemed to have a symbol on it like a brand and he tried to find out which designer it represented. Then one day he realised that the leaf bore the image of a loop.

That day Flare and Steele received a call from his housekeeper. They drove to his house and found Paul DeLonge hanging from a rope that had been hoisted over the wardrobe in his bedroom.

'It seems Marcus Floren got his way', Steele said.

'Was it a mistake?', Flare said.

'What do you mean?'

'He might have been into erotic asphyxiation, the Glamour Set had some strange sexual habits.'

He noticed Steele looked uncomfortable. They returned to the station, where the Sergeant told Flare he had found a crumpled leaf in Marcus Floren's cell.

'How did it get in there?', he said to Steele as he showed it to her. 'It looks like he's drawn a noose on it.'

Kester Floren was diagnosed as suffering from schizophrenia and committed to Broadmoor on the grounds that his connection with his psychopathic twin made him a danger.

'It seems beyond doubt', Don Harvard said, 'that he didn't know his brother was killing people.'

Nurses reported he would hold long conversations alone which he claimed were with his brother. He would clip articles and adverts from magazines about designer brands. He favoured Versace and Gucci and filled his room with images of them.

Marcus Floren was convicted of multiple murders by the Old Bailey and given several life sentences.

Throughout the trial he remained serene, and journalists noted the different faces he seemed to have in the shots they obtained of him. Reporters wrote that he looked every inch the groomed male of glossy magazines, an incongruous presence, as if the wrong man was attending court.

As soon as he arrived at Belmarsh prison he found reams of letters waiting for him from enamoured women. His model's looks and courteous intelligence found him favour with the guards and they allowed him to correspond with his female admirers.

Shortly after his imprisonment Marcus Floren claimed to be called Jack Martins and was sent to see the prison psychiatrist, Dr. Adam Grimes, who diagnosed multiple personality disorder. He noted that Marcus Floren's personality shifted during their sessions, and wrote: "even his face changes at times".

Marcus Floren enjoyed walking the shiny metal corridors watching the other prisoners.

'I shine my cell so it is a mirror', he told Dr. Grimes. 'I run Mirrorland. I am in contact with my brother, and the double I have created is outside, for the world of Glamour is a cannibalistic one'.

Dr. Grimes was interested in criminality among twins and asked what Marcus thought his brother was doing in Broadmoor.

'He is clipping the magazines I tell him to', Marcus said, 'if you don't believe me check the veracity of it.'

Dr. Grimes received a detailed report of the pages that filled Kester Floren's room. These were the same ones from the identical magazines that Marcus Floren has secreted behind the sink in his cell.

Shortly after this both twins were denied the privilege of reading materials. They seemed surprisingly unaffected. Dr. Grimes continued his sessions with Marcus Floren and found him to be a fascinating study in his subject. Marcus Floren gave him excellent culinary advice, reawakening in the doctor an old passion for gastronomy. He found great pleasure in making dishes for his wife, a bored demirep with too much time on her hands.

Le Feu was taken over by an up and coming chef who managed to use its notoriety for business. His restaurant was filled with celebrities. The booking time was months ahead.

And the Glamour Club found it had a new owner. He turned up there and set about filling it with models and many of the diners at Le Feu. He catered to the voyeurism of the men and women who flocked there.

Around this time Flare received a letter which read "There is one murder I committed that you don't know about." It was signed Marcus Floren.

He and Steele made their way to the prison on a day when a bright sun stood in a cloudless sky.

Marcus Floren was waiting for them and he looked directly at Steele as she entered.

'You say there is someone you killed who we don't know about', Flare said.

'Do you know the Glamour Club has been started up again? I get all sorts of communication in here. The new owner is exceptionally handsome and wears the finest clothes.'

'Have you brought us here to play a game?', Steele said.

He looked at her and she felt as if she was being absorbed by a reel of film.

'Jack Martins is alive', Marcus Floren said. 'It was not him but his identical twin Julian Martins who I killed. He had good brains. You saw his head in my fridge.'

'Another pair of twins', Flare said. 'You really are crazy.'

'There is a far higher incidence of identical twins than you know. You can check out the veracity of what I'm saying.'

'We will.'

'Julian was Jack's well kept secret. He had keys to Jack's flat. Jack occasionally asked him to sleep with one of the wives. He was furious with him when he found out Julian had syphilis.'

'How do you know all this?', Flare said.

'One night at Le Feu, Jack was unable to pay for drinks when he was stood up by the Glamour Set. I waived the debt and he told me of his brother, he told me everything as I filled his glass. Jack found out that Julian had screwed Samantha one evening when he was out. Julian used to go to his brother's flat to eat and drink, since he was always short of money. I followed the people I killed. I have a particular interest in Jack and had him under surveillance. He had been served an eviction notice. One afternoon as Jack lunched with Samantha, Julian went to his flat, packed the clothes he kept there, and headed to Heathrow. It was Julian I followed to Heathrow, it was Julian I killed.'

'Why did you spare Jack?', Steele said.

Marcus Floren looked at her and smiled.

'You're not very discerning where men are concerned, are you Detective Steele?', he said.

'Why spare Mirabelle Samson?', Flare said.

'She never went to the Glamour Club.'

'So what happened to Jack Martins?', Flare said.

'He returned to his flat shortly after his twin had left, and got a call from an old lover who had got divorced. She told him she'd done well out of her husband and invited him down to her country mansion. He took her up on the offer, leaving that afternoon.'

'How do you know?', Flare said.

'Because I've spoken to him.'

'Is there anything else you want to tell us?', Flare said.

'Over the ensuing weeks Jack used his charms to

secure a large loan from his lover. He used it to buy his way back into the Glamour Set. He saw 22 Hertford Street up for sale and promptly put in an offer. This was around the time he found he had a craving for animal organs.'

'Why your interest in the Glamour Club?', Flare said. 'You're going to be in here for life.'

'You think so? Who is Mr. Glamour? Come on, Chief Inspector Flare, do you know? Inspector Steele?'

'I think he's a symbol of what you wanted to be', Flare said. 'All the wealth and glitz you were so obsessed by.'

'He's out there, he has no interest in you, and Steele with her sexual hang ups. I can enter the mind of anyone.'

The guards moved in on him as he pulled it from his pocket.

Steele thought it was a knife, but she saw it was a small mirror he was holding up to them.

'See you in Mirrorland. Mr. Glamour is the reason I am not in prison', he said as they led him away.

It checked out. Birth records revealed Jack Martins had a twin named Julian.

'What has Jack Martins lost? A brother he didn't care for?', Steele said. 'It's almost as if he's complicit in it all.'

'Maybe he's Mr. Glamour', Flare said. 'Marcus, Kester and Jack, it's like some black trinity. And Marcus gets to run it all in his own mind. The King of his voyeuristic world.'

A few months later Marcus Floren got a job working in the kitchens of Belmarsh prison. He cleaned all the work surfaces until they shone like polished glass. One inmate saw Marcus's face in every corner of the room, in every steel surface. He thought Marcus was staring out of the knives, which looked like mirrors. He said Marcus was visiting him at night. He found a menu from Le Feu dated that week in his cell, which he showed to a bemused guard.

He was sent to the prison psychiatrist when he claimed that Marcus was cooking in designer clothes and filming everyone. He claimed he could hear female laughter and smell perfume amid the kitchen odours.

'Welcome to my world', Dr. Grimes said. 'I suggest you change your diet.'

The following day the prisoner's mutilated body was found in his locked cell. His side had been cut open. His cell mate said he saw nothing, heard nothing. It was the afternoon that Dr. Grimes's wife went missing.

That same week Jack Martins decided to diversify the menu at the Glamour Club. He set up an account with the butcher who supplied Le Feu.

And Flare and Steele received a package in the post. Analysis revealed the contents to be two human kidneys.

If you enjoyed Mr. Glamour then you might like these titles

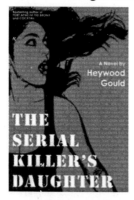

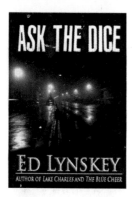

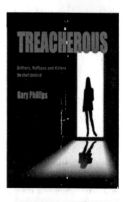

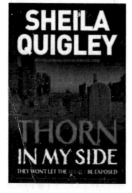